LEXI J. KINGSTON

COME
NIGHT
FALL

Published by L. Kingston Books, LLC
Edited by Susan Barnes
Cover Design by Lexi Kingston

❀ Created with Vellum

COME

NIGHT
FALL

For the wanderers.
The Lost.
The Found.
And those who haven't yet
decided which they are.
The mystery lies within us all.

CHAPTER 1

*R*ain splatters on the roof as the TV blares from the living room where my father sits, probably asleep, definitely drunk, and completely unaware that the annoying sound is keeping me and my brother awake. The flickering glow spills through the small cracks in my door, and the old wood is so desiccated that it not only creaks when moved, but pieces fall off as well.

The floors above me groan with the wind, and I've often wondered just how stable this house is, if the second floor is even sound to walk on. Father claims it's safe enough, but "safe enough" isn't comforting to me.

A soft whisper flows through the room as outside air rushes in through the cracked window, bringing with it a spray of rainwater. I wipe perspiration from my upper lip and flop over in bed, sparing a glance toward my brother's room, which looks straight into mine. There had been a door separating our conjoining rooms when we moved in, until he tripped and used it to catch himself—only to have it crash to the floor with him, breaking into a thousand, tiny pieces.

Just the same, the entrance to his room refuses to open, and I fear if it did, the entire foundation would fall, given how badly it groans every time someone attempts to un-jam it.

"I don't understand," I whisper, smoothing the strands of hair stuck to my face. "Why here?"

I close my eyes and wait for the answer I know will never come. I don't expect it to—it hasn't yet in the two weeks since we arrived. Though, I don't expect much of anything as of late. Mostly, I'm thankful I was given the softest of the three beds, something my father often finds reason to accuse me of: costing him a good night's sleep.

None of us were exactly happy about the move, nor were we thrilled at the idea of living here until "things get sorted out," which in our family seems to be never or in death... and I'm certainly not for the latter.

The rain picks up, pounding against my window with such force I spring from the bed, falling to the floor as I grapple with my sheets. A five-seven girl is not meant for a measly twin bed.

"Are you all right?" my brother whispers from the room beyond mine.

"Yes, yes, I'm fine," I whisper harshly in response. Father doesn't like to be woken up, especially with a half-empty bottle in his hand, so we try to keep our voices low.

"Are you sure?" He comes to stand in the open doorway. He should consider himself lucky our rooms are conjoining, or else he would have nowhere to sleep.

"I'm fine." I force a smile, meeting his eyes as I use my knee to rise tiredly from the floor. Braving the raging weather, I press both hands firmly on the windowpane, shoving it down with all my might. It squeals in protest, slowly obeying. "Truly."

He wrings his hands, taking small, tentative steps toward

me before he changes his mind and sits on the floor, resting his back against the side of my squeaky bed. I fall onto the mattress, taking a heavy breath of dense, stifling air so thick that bedsheets are unnecessary. "You know, this—"

"Is only temporary," I recite. "I know."

"Good. I think Mom is worried it's more than that," he admits, pulling his knees to his chest.

I brush the sweaty, ash-coated hair from his forehead—the downside of being in the room that's home to an open fireplace, everything is so filthy it's almost unlivable. He looks up at me, a fake smile painted on his lips. It hasn't been real for some time now, but then again, mine hasn't either.

"You're hotter than me," I accuse. "Bring your mattress in here for the night. Hopefully the repairman will be here to fix the air-conditioner in the morning."

He nods and drags his mattress between rooms, placing it next to the broken bed frame Father tried to salvage and couldn't. Though, you can hardly call a few pieces of tape an honest effort.

So much about our lives has changed, but the difference in his personality is the most noticeable... right next to Mom's.

"I don't want to live like this," I admit, and for a moment, I fear he's already fallen asleep until I hear a heavy sigh.

"It's only temporary," he reminds me, pulling the lamp cord so the room erupts in a dim, orange glow. He's never particularly liked the dark. Well, not since—

"Get some sleep," he instructs, wrapping the covers around himself like a cocoon.

"You first," I challenge, and he snickers softly.

At a certain point, I begin to wonder how temporary this

state of temporality is. And how long until our only hope of leaving becomes a temporary promise as well.

"Goodnight, Aspen," my brother whispers, rolling over so his back is facing me.

"Goodnight, Dallas."

~

There's a heavy pounding at the front door, and I startle awake, clutching my chest as if that alone might calm my pounding heart.

"What the hell was that?" I ask, wondering who on earth would bother anyone at this hour, let alone us—the strange neighbors who recently moved into the decrepit house. Besides the previous squatters and kids who broke in for the thrill, no one ventures this far down our dead-end road. It was obvious when we moved in that this place hadn't been as empty as we'd thought, given the number of footprints we found littering the entryway, but oddly enough, they never went any farther than that.

"Well? Any ideas?" I accuse, knowing all too well the kinds of trouble my brother can find himself in. "Dallas?"

I turn to where he sleeps on my floor—keyword being *sleeps*. The pounding must not have woken him up, though it's hard to tell through the darkness. He's normally such a light sleeper, too, and it's unlike him to turn off the lamp.

The pounding comes again, and I look back to where my brother lies unmoving, unshaken by the angry booming at the front door. I move through the room and grasp the decaying bedroom door, opening it slowly so as not to give any indication that there's someone here, or at least, someone awake.

As I tiptoe slowly through the shadows and TV light, my eyes find a lump, face-down on the couch—my father—still snoring and completely unaffected by the knocking. It's not uncommon for him to sleep through lots of noise, given the state of his coherency is typically pretty low, if present at all. Still, waking him up is not something I ever want to do.

I keep to the walls as I walk through the living room, careful to avoid passing any windows too closely. I drop to my knees as the banging continues, crawling quietly to the door where a small crack reveals the outside. My clammy fingers grasp the surface as I pull myself to a standing position, my nightgown catching beneath my feet.

Bang, bang, bang.

I swallow hard, forcing myself to keep my breathing quiet and even.

Never let the enemy see your fear.

It's a new town, a new neighborhood, so it wouldn't be out of place for onlookers to snoop, or even attempt to scare the newcomers.

When I glance through the crack in the door, all I see is the glow of our neighbor's porch lights shimmering off the ground, damp with puddles from the rain. Very few people live around us, and those that do are mostly hidden from view by the thick of trees between houses.

My chest rises and falls slowly as my fingers clutch and twist the door handle, opening the creaky door as slowly as possible to get a better look outside. I'm fully aware of how stupid this is—there might still be someone out there that I can't see—but for some reason, I'm compelled to find out who it is.

Gradually, I peek my head out to find, just as before, that there's no one in sight. There are no signs of life anywhere actually, which is strange considering those pesky raccoons are always traipsing through our garbage, raking it up and leaving it all across the yard.

"Hello?" I call out into the night. I squint my eyes through the darkness, looking for the culprit who has kept me up and paranoid for so long. "I know someone's there."

Something in the distance moves rapidly, so fast I can't follow. My eyes dart around the yard and my hands tremble as the wind picks up, blowing leaves toward me and through the cracked front door.

"Shit," I curse, knowing perfectly well that I'll have to wait until morning to clean them up in the light.

"Hello?" I call out one last time, deciding that maybe my eyes are playing tricks on me. The annoyance banging on our door is long gone, probably asleep in his own bed now that his nightly tormenting is finished. But as I'm closing the door, a gust of wind blows against it with so much force that I can't shut it. I've never felt wind so strong, almost like someone was pushing from the other side.

"What in the world?" I gasp, allowing the door to slam back open. I grimace at the damage it's probably done to the doorframe and pray that it's not broken in the morning—we have enough repairs to do as it is. I twist around, glancing at my father's still frame on the couch, thankfully, still asleep.

I breathe a sigh of relief, and just as abruptly as it started, the wind stops. Except this time, when I look out the door, something glimmering against the porch catches my eye. I step outside in nothing but my nightgown and bravery, or maybe stupidity—I've yet to decide which—and bend, running my fingers over the small chain that holds a heart-shaped pendant. It's faded with vines snaking up the surface, looking to be centuries old—not that I know anything about that sort of stuff. Mom used to. Before.

Grabbing the necklace, I stand and turn to go inside so I can examine it closer, but just then, the front door slams, knocking me back a few steps. A scream erupts from deep in my throat, and I lurch forward, twisting the knob and giving it a shove.

"No, no, no!" I ram my shoulder into the door with all of my strength. Leaves swirl around me like a dream, and the nearby trees groan in protest of the bossy winds.

Heat trickles down my neck, warmer than the humid air surrounding me and noticeably different than the harsh breeze. My heart pounds in my chest, and I squeeze the necklace tightly, as if the thing placed to lure me out into the open might be my savior.

My teeth gnaw at my lip as I turn slowly to find a figure standing before me. Too close. His eyes are black as the night and his hot breath surrounds me, choking me, calling me.

"We've been waiting for you, Aspen," he whispers, a ghostly smile overtaking his face.

I scream loud enough to wake the entire neighborhood.

CHAPTER 2

I bolt upright in bed, clutching my chest with both hands as sweat soaks into my hair and clothes.

"Bad dream?" Dallas calls from his closet where he stands with his shirtless back to me. He rummages through his small selection of t-shirts before pulling a red one over his head, then turns, cocking his head to the side. "Aspen? Don't tell me you've seen a ghost already. I told Father there are probably creepy crawlies among us in this wretched place."

My eyes are wide as I take in the room. Everything is as it was when I fell asleep last night. The lamp is still on. The window is closed.

Throwing off my covers, I run to the front door to find it's closed and locked as though nothing is out of the ordinary. Like nothing happened last night. I examine the frame for scratches or dents, any cracks or missing chunks. Nothing. It's exactly as it was yesterday—barely functioning, but also the only sturdy thing in our little shack.

My spine tingles as the feeling of hot breath seeps down my

neck. My heart rate picks up and I brace myself for what's to come. To see that ghostly face again.

"Aspen." Dallas's hand squeezes my shoulder , and I jump, brushing him off with clammy fingers.

"Don't sneak up on me like that!" I yell, causing my father to snort and stir on the couch. Dallas pins me with a meaningful look.

"I'm sorry. But I just had the most bizarre night. There was this banging, and—and this man. Dallas, I've never seen anyone like him. It was so odd. Are you sure nothing woke you up?"

"Are you having nightmares again?" he asks, placing his thumb under my chin so I'm forced to look at him. His disheveled hair sticks up at odd angles, and his brown eyes look desperate for a full night's rest.

"No, of course not. Trust me, you'd know. Besides, this wasn't like that. There was a man knocking at the door, you didn't hear anything?"

"Like I said before, I slept through the whole night for the first time in a while actually."

"Breakfast?"

We both turn toward our mom, dressed in the only thing she's worn since the accident—a long nightgown with ruffles on the shoulders. Never does she change into day clothes or do her makeup like before. She simply switches between the light pink one or another in light blue.

"No, Mom, we're not hungry," Dallas speaks for both of us, stirring my irritation.

"I'm starving. Mom, would you like any help?"

She smiles at my offer, removing her apron and draping it over my neck.

She places her hands on my cheeks, patting them with

affection. "What a beautiful girl you are. You remind me so much of Rachel when she was your age." A longing expression crosses her face, and for a moment, she's Mom again—stressed, run-down, always busy, always with a weight on her shoulders.

"Mom," Dallas warns, resting a hand on her side.

"Right. Right. We are not to speak her name." She closes her eyes to regain her composure, the plastered smile retaking its rightful place on her lips. "Now, let's not live in the past. Aspen, dear, scramble the eggs for me, will you?"

"'Course, Mom." I swallow, holding back a wave of tears.

She has been like this for months. Sometimes we're lucky enough to catch a glimpse of the mom we knew, the one who raised us, who read us bedtime stories despite working sixteen hours and needing sleep of her own. The mom who cooked us breakfast and drove us to school every morning without complaint.

I watch as she busies herself at the stove, the only place I see her nowadays except lying in bed when she has a "bad day."

This is the first good one she's had in almost a month.

"Don't talk about your nightmares in front of Mom. You might send her spiraling again," Dallas warns, squeezing my arm.

"I'm telling you, it was real." I will him to listen, but he dismisses me, raising his eyebrows in denial. I close my eyes and swallow, shaking my head rapidly. "Or at least it felt real. Dallas, I have a bad feeling. It was wrong. Something's wrong."

His dubious expression only irritates me further. "So apparently bad dreams are omens now?"

"You know better than to ignore my gut feelings," I remind him, cracking an egg and letting its contents drop into the bowl with the others Mom has already scrambled... shells and all.

Dallas's expression darkens, and he takes a step toward me, voice low. "That was completely different and you know it. That was *real*. We are talking about your dreams here, Aspen."

"Which doesn't make my apprehension any less valid. I'm telling you—"

"Aspen, you said you'd help." Mom beckons me over to the stovetop, motioning for me to finish scrambling the eggs.

"Sorry, Mom." I shoot Dallas an irritated look.

"Now, if you two could get along for five seconds, I'd be overjoyed." She clicks her tongue, twisting her hair into a high ponytail that brushes the top of her thin, bony shoulders.

"Sorry, Mom," we say simultaneously, then glare at one another. Mom pauses her kitchen duties to touch each of our faces, something she used to do when we were kids.

"Don't be sorry, loves. Now, Dallas, help with the pancakes." She nudges his chin affectionately with her thumb, then rests her eyes on me. They slowly trail down my face and to my chest, where they linger. "Well, dear, that's a lovely necklace. Where did you find it?"

Nausea rolls through my stomach like a tidal wave.

Necklace?

I turn to face the circular, antique mirror on the wall—one of the only things we brought with us from home. My eyes rest on the short, gold chain clinging to my skin like a tattoo. I clear my throat several times, opening and closing my mouth in order to come up with some excuse as to why it's around my neck.

"It was only a dream," I remind my paranoia. Then the mirror morphs, and the face of the stranger stares back at me with those same soulless eyes and unholy smile. Chills run down my spine, even as sweat drips down my face from the eighty-degree weather and our lack of air conditioning. He seems to be beckoning me, calling me to him, and all I want to do is scream at him to leave me alone. I'm about to do just that when my mom speaks.

"What was a dream?" she inquires, that fake, petulant smile never wavering. She's a drone. A mirror image of the woman she once was. She's the shell of an egg after it's been cracked and emptied of its yolk. That's my mother—hollow. Empty. Broken.

It sickens me.

I can't find the words to express what I'm feeling. What I'm seeing. How does a necklace I dreamt about end up clasped around my neck? The only logical explanation is that it wasn't a dream at all, though I'm not sure how to convince anyone else of that without being accused of losing my mind.

Dallas speaks before I do, soothing Mom's poor attempt at worrying, but I don't hear what he says. The necklace entrances me, and I find myself taking small steps toward the mirror to get a better look. The man fades in and out of view as I get closer. One moment it's his pale, unsmiling face staring back at me, and the next it's mine.

My fingers brush the cool pendant resting on my chest, and I notice just how heavy it is. Heavy enough that I should have noticed it the moment I woke up this morning. Instead, I'd been too concerned with what may or may not have happened last night.

Reaching up toward the mirror, I find that his face is gone again, leaving only my own ghostly expression. When my fingers make contact with the glass, it sparks, causing me to jump back. A thin, barely visible crack snakes diagonally across the mirror, not stopping until it stretches from corner to corner.

"You saw that, right?" I turn breathlessly to Dallas, who watches me with morbid curiosity.

He blinks several times, searching my expression. "I saw you staring strangely at the mirror... if that's what you mean?"

"No, you doofus, the crack." I point at the center of the mirror, running my finger over the jagged line. "Look."

Dallas investigates the mirror, and Mom moves closer to do the same. "What a shame. It must have cracked during the move," she whispers, brushing her fingers across it longingly. I've never understood why the mirror means so much to her. It's an ugly piece of junk in my opinion.

When she walks away, I grab Dallas's arm before he can follow. "The mirror didn't crack during the move. It wasn't like that before. It cracked when I touched it."

He looks at me like I've lost my mind. "I'm fairly sure we would have seen the mirror crack when you touched it. Go help Mom, and stop acting bizarre. You know how it affects her."

"Aren't you going to listen to me?" I hiss, but he's already walking up the stairs toward the study, where he spends most of his time reading science fiction novels about things crazier than this. You'd think he, of all people, would believe me.

Especially after everything we've been through.

In the bathroom, I stare at my reflection. My fingers fiddle with the clasp of the necklace, but as soon as I unhook it, I reattach the ends. Dropping my hands, I touch the pendant briefly before deciding against removing it. There's no reason to keep wearing it, but there's also no real reason not to. Not really.

I can't explain it, but for some reason I don't feel right taking it off.

Giving up, I head back toward my bedroom to lie down. With nothing better to do, I stare at the ceiling and replay the events of last night over and over again until Father stirs in the living room.

As per usual, he isn't in the happiest of moods, especially when he realizes the last of his beer is gone. I listen as he rants and raves to no one in particular, blaming Dallas for drinking it all with his friends. Granted, that's how my brother went about life back home, poking around in Father's liquor cabinet for something strong enough for a good time, but what he forgets is neither of us have friends here. Eventually, he yells for me to go into town for more beer.

The past few times he asked, I've managed to convince Dallas to make the trip for me. In fact, he usually offers, claiming he needs to get out of this stuffy house. Except this time, when I tell him what Father has asked of me, he shrugs his shoulders and tells me to take the road path and not the short cut through the woods.

"You don't want to go for me?" I ask, trying and failing to hold his attention for more than a few seconds at a time.

Finally, he sighs and sets his pen down on the dirty, ripped up tablecloth beneath his lined paper. He used to write on his computer, but he had to leave that behind in the move. We had to leave everything but the clothes on our backs and the items closest to us that we could grab. "You can't avoid going into town forever."

I shake my head, fear and anxiety settling in my chest. "Well then, come with me. Please, I don't know where anything is."

Dallas turns, his full attention on me at last. The muted light from the small, round window casts a shadow over half of his face, making him look wicked. He puts both of his hands on my shoulders, giving them a slight squeeze as he releases a breath. "Once you get into town, it's the first shop on the right with the blue roof. You can't miss it, Aspen. You'll be fine."

"But—"

"Nothing bad will happen to you if you leave the house." He eases from his chair before pulling me to his chest in a tight hug. "You can't be afraid forever."

"I think we both know I can be," I mumble against the fabric of his t-shirt while attempting to fight off the trembling in my hands.

CHAPTER 3

*T*he walk into town is long and grueling and it doesn't help that I take my time, hoping at any moment Dallas might emerge from the house, informing me he's changed his mind and I don't have to go alone.

He never does. He just watches through the window with a somber expression as I leave.

"Just brilliant." I curse under my breath, adjusting the bag on my shoulder that I've brought for groceries. We don't currently have a car, having left it at an abandoned parking lot near the airport back home. Father says we'll buy one eventually, but until then, we're forced to walk wherever we want to go. Not that it really matters. This town is small enough to walk from one end to the other in under thirty minutes.

The sun casts a gloomy light upon our small neighborhood, but most of the rays are blocked by the tall trees overhead that sway softly in the wind. Creaks sound from the old wood, and I quicken my pace after remembering the last time I heard trees moan like that.

The chain around my neck grows heavier with each step I take, and I can feel it weighing down on my chest like a thousand bricks. I'm not entirely sure why I didn't remove it the second Mom pointed it out to me, but for some reason, I couldn't.

As I'm walking down the small, brick pathway, I notice a clearing up ahead, and—thank God almighty—a blue roof.

Relief sweeps through me, and I release a heavy sigh. That wasn't nearly as hard as I made it out to be in my head. I continue walking until I'm in front of the small store and push on the bent screen door.

"Good afternoon, Miss. What can I get for ya?" A short, thick man greets from behind the counter, holding a towel that I presume is used for wiping beads of sweat off of his round, shiny head. Skin pudges just below his chin, and the folds jiggle on his thick neck as he moves around the counter.

"A four pack of Stella Artois," I reply, giving him a smile. It's amazing he has any alcohol to sell, given it looks as though most of it ends up in his gut.

Back home, our distributors didn't check IDs or question you if you looked a tad too young because everyone knew everyone. But here, no one knows me. Come to think of it, I'm not entirely sure of the legal drinking age here.

"That'll be nine pounds." He holds his sausage fingers out for money, and as soon as I drop it into his damp hand, careful not to brush against him, he pockets the change. "Have a nice day now."

He waves, smiling at me with rotten, smoker's teeth. A wink follows, and I find myself walking faster and faster out the door.

"You as well," I mutter, only breathing when I'm out in the open with dozens of cheery faces surrounding me.

Townspeople roam around the outdoor market, and fruit carts line the road as far as I can see, filled to the brims with apples, bananas, and oranges ripe to perfection. The sight is overwhelming to my hungry stomach, which yearns for the breakfast I skipped earlier.

It's so... homey. Inviting. The total and complete opposite of the dark and dreary block of broken wood I now call a home. This little town is beautiful in a quaint sort of way, and I say a silent thank you to my brother for forcing me to come alone. If he were here, he'd rush me so he could get back to working on his masterpiece, which he still won't let me have a peek at.

There's a small, pink charm bracelet on a nearby stand that captures my attention. Mom would have loved it. Before.

After picking up a few pieces of fruit, I make my way to the table. There's no line, so I walk straight up to it, browsing the array of bracelets that are neatly laid out, but I only have eyes for the one.

"Hello dear, how can I help you?" a small, gray-haired lady asks me with a warm and welcoming smile. She wears a blue and white knitted dress that hangs off of her round shoulders, down past her small, stubby knees.

"The pink bracelet, please." I point behind her. My mom used to have one just like it as a kid, and if she were feeling like herself, I know she'd appreciate the gift. "The one with the gold charm."

The lady removes the bracelet from its hook, and gently lays it in my hand.

"Be careful with this one. It's very old." She closes my fingers around it, giving them a squeeze.

"Thank you, I will. Where did you get all of these?" I wonder, curious as to how one person simply stumbles across a collection of jewelry so divine.

She waves her hand, dismissing my question. "Oh here, there, everywhere. A lot of it belonged to my ancestors, and it's not doing me much good sitting in the ol' attic now is it?"

"No, I guess not." I laugh softly, anticipating a price. When she simply blinks without another word, I ask, "How much is it?"

The woman laughs, shaking her head like I'm silly. "Don't you worry about it, hon. It's on me. Welcome to the neighborhood."

She provides me with a small, white gift bag and wraps the bracelet in baby pink tissue paper.

I thank her and prepare to leave, but there's still no one in line behind me, and I've had a question burning in the back of my mind since I saw the unique jewelry display.

"Can I ask you something?"

"Of course." She smiles kindly as a look of open curiosity morphs her features.

A thin layer of sweat coats my palms as I reach around my neck to unclasp the necklace. I hold it out to her. "Have you ever sold anything like this?"

The woman, Edna, I gather from her name tag, runs her fingers over the heart pendant, stroking it as though enough love and care will tell her where it's from.

She shakes her head slowly, still inspecting its twisting design. "I can't say I've ever seen anythin' like it. Where'd you find a gorgeous thing like this?"

Telling her I found it in a dream and woke up with it around my neck is out of the question, so I settle for the closest thing to the truth. "I found it on my porch when we moved in. It was lodged between the wood."

"That sure is an odd place for a necklace that's not the least bit tarnished. Though, you are living in that old thing, and nothing good has ever been known to come out of there." Edna's eyes widen when she realizes what she's said. "Until now, of course. You and your family just might be the blessing we need to rid the town of the Draven Home of Horrors stories."

"That's... comforting." I swallow, suddenly eager to get my necklace back and abandon this town for good.

My stomach churns. Small town or not, how could this woman possibly know who I am and where I live? I don't leave the house very often, and I've never seen her before in my life.

"If you'd like," she offers, rolling her sleeves up to her elbows, revealing old, frail arms covered in wrinkles and freckles, as well as a small cross tattoo, "I could hold onto it for you and do a little research."

"That's all right." I reach for the necklace, afraid if I don't, she won't return it. "Thank you, though."

For scaring the shit out of me, I add silently.

The last thing I wanted to know was that the house I'm currently living in is known as the Draven Home of Horrors. Who wants to be told their new home is a small town's source of supernatural excitement?

Although, that would better explain why someone was messing with me last night, even if the necklace doesn't fit with that theory. There's also the grave possibility that all of this is my overactive imagination trying to make sense of the new life I'm living.

I thank Edna one last time and move on. I should go home and give Father his beer, but I can't bring myself to leave just yet. He waited forty-seven years to become an alcoholic. He can wait a little longer to get his fix.

"Could you maybe watch where you're going?" a voice accuses as my shoulder slams into hers. I back away swiftly, clutching the groceries to my chest.

"I'm so sorry." I assess the girl before me—long dark hair, full ruby red lips, and an outfit that puts my tank top and denim cut-off shorts to shame. Her skin is pale, so white it's almost porcelain, unlike my pasty legs and dirty blonde hair, darkened from lack of sun in the mountains of Colorado. The girl crosses her arms, looking down on me with disgust.

"I hate newcomers," she grumbles, turning on the balls of her feet. My jaw drops at her rudeness, and I'm forced to lean backward to avoid getting a mouthful of hair when she turns on the balls of her feet and struts away. I didn't expect everyone to be welcoming and friendly, but *wow*.

"Don't mind her." Another female voice surprises me, making me swivel around once more. "She's the queen of being overdramatic. Just be glad she didn't tell you to 'know your place.'"

My eyes rest on yet another pretty, yet much more approachable girl. Her complexion brighter and her welcoming blue eyes instantly put me at ease.

"She doesn't even know me," I scoff, extending my hand to her.

"You're Aspen," she says without hesitation, and it takes her a moment to recognize my discomfort. How is it that both she and Edna seem to know who I am already? Even the rude girl referred to me as a newcomer. "Everyone here knows you. You're new. Probably the newest family to move here since, well, way before I was born. I'm Elaine. Elaine Graves."

"Nice to meet you." My nerves subside when she shakes my hand. "Does everyone know everyone around here?"

"Oh, yes. Small town drama is definitely a thing as well. I'm sure you've already been filled in by Edna over there about the legends around your house?" She brushes her auburn hair from her shoulders, rolling her aqua eyes.

"I've heard more than I'd like, honestly." I should be used to this sort of atmosphere because of where I lived before, but I'd kind of hoped to escape the small town politics and just blend in for once.

"I'm sure. This is your fresh start, you don't want to be held back by old myths."

I nod in agreement, shifting the grocery bag to my shoulder because my arms are getting tired. Elaine is still talking, but my attention shifts back to the rude girl and what looks to be her... friends? Family? It's hard to tell from here.

For the most part, they all have the same dark hair and sculpted features, pure white skin, paler than I've ever seen, and an air about them that I can't quite describe. They feel important. Too important for a town this size.

"Who are they?" I wonder softly, interrupting my possibly-new-friend. Not the best way to thank her for her generosity, but I can't help it. Even as she responds, my attention never strays from the enchanting family

"They're the Dravens," she mocks, her own attention now captured by their mysterious beauty. "The family your house was named after. The one who ran into you was Vira. Consider yourself lucky all you got was a stern talking to—the last guy she flipped on wound up with a broken hand."

"Why are they so..."

"Perfect?" she snarks before glancing away quickly when one of them notices us staring. "If I knew their secrets, do you think I'd be living here instead of traveling the world and posing for magazine covers?"

I refrain from telling her she could already do that if she wanted, and focus instead on each of them individually. "And they're all related?"

She nods, and I fear she might start drooling any minute. "There are six of them, not including the parents, and then there's their 'clan' as Oliver and I like to call them—Oliver's my best friend. Did you leave any friends behind when you moved?"

Her attention span must be that of a fly to move so swiftly between topics. "No, not really. My brother's always been the one who makes friends. Not me."

That's not technically true. We lived in one place my entire life, and just like here, there weren't many newcomers to befriend, which I assume is why Elaine is latching on to me. She's in need of a fresh face. I used to have friends, but after years of drama and disappointment, I pushed them all away. I spent time with Dallas and his friends instead, whenever they'd come over. Luckily, I have a great brother who didn't mind me tagging along, but he didn't bring them around all that often, which left me to my bedroom with nothing but music and my thoughts.

"Well then, you'll fit in just fine with me and Oliver." I smile, but she must not take it as sincere, because she backs off a little. "I apologize if I'm being too pushy. It's just, we don't have much variety around here and the most exciting thing that happens is, well, seeing the Dravens outside of their manor."

I shake my head, stopping her. "Don't worry, I'm in need of some friends. Maybe even a little excitement."

"Good." She smirks mischievously. "It gets boring around here, so we have to make our own fun."

I nod absently as my eyes drift back to the family. "Tell me more about the Dravens."

Her brows lift, and her gaze follows mine. "You sure are curious."

"Oh. No, I just—" I stumble on my words. Honestly, I'm just trying to figure out why my house has such a bad reputation, other than its terrible condition.

"Hey, it's okay. I would be too if I'd never seen anyone who looked like that before." Elaine then proceeds to discreetly point to each of them, naming them one by one. "Well, you've already been acquainted with Vira. The tall one next to her is Elliot." She nods toward the boy closest to us, his arms more muscular than I've ever seen on someone our age. "He's the oldest. The one next to him with the pin-straight black hair is Vanesa—she looks sweet, but I hear she's a viper just like Vira."

I take them in one by one. They're all similar looking, but very distinctive in the way they carry themselves—some with confidence and others with arrogance.

"Then there's Danielle with the short hair and black skirt." Unlike Vanesa and Vira, who are curvy and lanky, Danielle is slim and petite with a look of pure innocence. Her pale lips aren't as bold as her sisters' red and black ones, and her hair is more childish, pulled up in a half ponytail that shows off her round face and big, golden eyes. "She's the youngest, as well as Lucas, who is prodding at her for attention."

"Lucas looks different than the others," I say, noticing his blonde hair, which clashes with the other siblings' dark shades.

"He does. I think he might be adopted, but I'm not sure," she says thoughtfully, looking him up and down. "Anyway, the last one off to the right is Miles."

He's standing slightly apart from the group, not partaking in their laughter and teasing, just watching them with disinterest, as if there's nothing worth being a part of. "The lot of them are kind of cultish if you ask me, and the rest of the locals won't admit it, but they think so, too. Everyone stays away from the Dravens, and just as well, they keep to themselves. Their ancestors helped found our town, so they're kind of a big deal around here."

"Which of them lived in the house before my family?" I ask the question that's been at the forefront of my mind.

Elaine picks up an orange, tossing it between her hands mindlessly. "None of them that I know of. Actually, that house has been empty all my life except for a few stupid kids breaking in for the thrill of it. The townsfolk love a good legend, especially one they can experience."

"So, what's the legend?"

"You ask a lot of questions, don't you? Look, it's nothing you should be worried about. As far as anyone knows, nothing bad has ever actually happened in your house. They're just stories. So don't put too much thought into the things that go bump in the night."

"Honey, either put it back or buy it," the woman behind the cart barks, and Elaine abruptly places the orange back where she got it from.

"Sorry, Roseanne."

The woman grumbles something unintelligible under her

breath as we walk away giggling. "Rosie over there is not much of a people person, if you hadn't noticed."

"I gathered as much," I remark, astounded by the wide variety of personalities this little town holds. They go from mellow to extreme awfully fast, and a little too quickly for me to keep up with. "Look, I should probably get home, but it was nice meeting you."

"I can walk with you," Elaine offers, nodding toward the brick road that leads to the end of my street. "I live a little way up the road from you."

It's only a ten-minute walk, but the secluded, overgrown area does nothing for my paranoid imagination, and I was in no way looking forward to walking home alone. The groaning trees and whistling winds are so loud you would never know if someone was truly following you or if it was just nature cooing. "That would be great, thanks."

She nods, and when we start the trek home, I turn one last time to soak in the mystery that is the Draven family. What's stranger is that one of them is looking back at me. Our eyes meet, and I pause, allowing Elaine to move a few paces ahead of me.

His gaze feels hot like the burning sun, and only my intrigue keeps me from ducking and running in the opposite direction. Miles Draven holds me in a trance for so long it feels like hours before Elaine's voice drags me out of my lucid state.

"I thought you said you didn't know any of the Dravens?" she asks, sounding far away.

"I don't." My voice comes out dreamily, like I've been hypnotized, and a fog of confusion swims around in my head. Miles's dark hair blows as the wind picks up suddenly, leaves and dirt sweeping and swirling around us like a hurricane. In an instant, I blink and Miles is gone, along with the rest of his strange family.

"Aspen." Elaine tugs lightly on my arm, pulling me toward her.

"Sorry," I say, glancing back to where the Dravens were moments ago as Elaine drags me away from town. Dark clouds cover every inch of the sky, and I blink in confusion, unsure when the sun went in. She watches me warily, and I suck on my bottom lip, turning away from her questioning stare. "Was it really that strange?"

She shrugs. "No, not really. It's just, the Dravens don't normally associate with anyone other than each other and their close friends. They all live in the same section of town and don't bother extending their attention to anyone else."

"Then why was he looking at me?" I ask as images of last night and the necklace dance across my vision. They're not related. It wasn't even his face that I saw.

Though, it was someone who looks a lot like him. Could the person at my door have been a Draven? No, that's not possible if we saw the entire family, excluding the parents. The man last night was much too young to father children this old.

"I don't know," she says thoughtfully, for once not having all of the answers. "I mean, you are new. He's probably just baffled to see a fresh face around town. Maybe he didn't know you were coming?"

"Didn't everyone know? I mean, from what you said before, it sounded like it." And I have a feeling the Dravens have a way of finding out things, despite keeping themselves secluded from the rest of town.

"It's definitely strange," she says, more to herself than to me.

Our footsteps echo off the brick pavers, and as we walk, a thin layer of fog forms around our ankles.

"I didn't realize the weather here was so crazy," I say, attempting to change the subject to something other than that odd family. I don't want her to go and tell the town I'm obsessed with them.

"It normally isn't," she says, again, more as an inner thought. "Do you have any plans tomorrow?"

I shake my head. "This is the first time I've left the house since we moved in."

"Perfect. Let's meet up. I can show you around a little and introduce you to Oliver. He's been cooped up in his room all summer with homework—online classes—so I'm sure he'd love to get out of the house, too." She stops in front of a modest house with brown paint chipping off the exterior. "This is me."

I practically leap at her offer, thrilled to be meeting yet another person, making these two more friends than I had back home. "Yeah, that sounds great."

"Okay, then. I'll see you tomorrow, Aspen." Elaine gives me a tiny wave, backing up her front steps. "Oh, and welcome to Ichorye."

With that, she leaves me to walk the next three minutes alone. It's nowhere near sunset, but it's like an eternal pit of darkness in this part of town compared to the open area I've just come from. The closer I get to my destination, the thicker the trees are and the harder the wind blows. It grows darker and darker until only small strokes of sunlight break through the shelter of the trees.

I walk as swiftly as I can home, not once stopping to investigate the twigs snapping behind me or the shadows I glimpse in my peripheral vision. I have an eerie feeling that I'm being followed, so I pick up my pace and break into a run. By the time I reach my house, my legs feel like rubber, and I'm panting and out of breath.

I thrust open the front door, then swiftly close and lock it behind me.

"How the hell did it take you so long to get me a pack of beer?" Father barks from the couch the second I'm inside. There's a cold compress pressed to his forehead to help keep him calm. Mom sits on the rocking chair, smile wavering enough for me to know he's been having a meltdown for a while.

"Sorry," I say shortly. "But I met a girl in town, and I didn't want to run off right away and have her think I'm rude."

"You could have called," Mom says sweetly.

I breathe slowly to avoid snapping at her. "My phone is broken, remember? You guys promised you'd take me to get it repaired when we got here. I don't like wandering around alone without one."

Father grabs the beer from my hands, cracking open the first of many. "You know how I get when I don't have a drink in my hand."

"Coherent?" I grumble, dropping down next to him on the couch. He knows the drill and passes me a bottle. This is the best time to talk to my father, when he's not yet drunk, but also not not craving alcohol anymore. He's in the perfect state of bliss. "I've been wondering, who owned this place before us?"

Father blinks, momentarily baffled. "I suppose no one. It has been vacant for at least a hundred years."

I'm forced to hold my tongue to avoid making any snarky comments about the condition of our house. I don't want him to get mad and shut down. There aren't many opportunities to talk to him like this. "Yeah, but who did we buy it from?"

"It was in the family." He takes a long sip of beer and chokes, clutching his chest and bending forward. He always does this—gulps more than his mouth can hold. I rub his back until the coughing subsides, then continue on with my inquiry.

"In the family? I didn't know we had any relatives here?"

"We did a long time ago. I didn't know about the house until your grandfather passed and I discovered the deed. I'm not even sure he knew he had it."

"Then why did a Draven live here?"

"Is that name supposed to mean something to me?"

I sigh in defeat. "No, I guess not."

"Based on the records, I think this house was rented out to people all over town. It was their own version of a hotel since the town was too small and too far off the map to be a destination spot. It was rumored that a lot of secret business deals and affairs took place under this very roof."

"I guess they had to find some way to hold on to their secrets in a tell-all-town this small," I reason. "Did anyone keep records of the residents over the years."

Father pauses, and the beer's rim teases his bottom lip. "I wouldn't call them records, but I think I saw a list of names scribbled down somewhere in a box of your grandfather's things."

"Can I look?" I ask eagerly, scooting to the edge of the seat.

He sighs. "Tomorrow, Aspen. I don't feel like digging them out right now."

And if I know my father, he won't feel like digging them out tomorrow either.

Dallas rounds the corner, shaking his head like a dog and

drying it with a towel. "Hot water's almost gone, you might want to shower now."

I nod as he passes through the living room, knowing my time with our father is wearing thin as his patience.

"One more thing. Please," I beg, pursing my lips.

He lounges back against the couch, propping his feet on the coffee table. "Five seconds."

"Did you ever see this pendant on any images or paperwork for the house?" I hold up my necklace, close enough to his face that he doesn't have to move to see it.

"Yeah, actually. It's all over the papers. Every one of them. I assumed it was the logo for his business or something."

"Yeah." I take a deep breath, swallowing my unease. "Or something."

CHAPTER 4

*S*hades of black and white color my vision as I peer through the dark. I rub the sleep from my eyes and groan. Is it not possible for me to sleep through the night just once? Dallas is in his own room tonight since the humidity has subsided, courtesy of the abrupt wind storm earlier today... or yesterday, given it's two in the morning.

My heart jumps from my chest, and I inhale sharply. Two in the morning.

I think back to last night, and in my mind, I see flashes of the clock on my nightstand—two a.m.

No. Not again. Please, *not again.*

It must be a coincidence. My heart cannot handle another night like the last.

Panic takes over, and my body goes into a state of numbness, unable to move. My chest aches as my heart smashes into it. I try to move my toes, but I can't. My fingers are just as useless, only jerking slightly when I attempt to wiggle them. I close my eyes and will myself to breathe. It's only a nightmare. This is not real. Nothing can hurt you in a dream.

Nothing can hurt you in a dream.

The tingling sensation subsides, and I open my eyes slowly, taking in the darkness surrounding me. I couldn't see my hand in front of my face if I tried. Dallas must have turned off his lamp again.

My eyes skate past the window, and my blood turns to ice. A tall, shadowy figure stands inside my room, silhouette reflected in the moonlight cast through the window.

No. No, no, no, no. I don't need to see his face to know he's the man from last night. The one who's been waiting for me.

"Please go away," I whisper, silent tears streaming down my cheeks. "I'll give you your necklace back," I offer, though I'm not sure that's what he wants. After all, he led me to it to begin with.

"Aspen…" he whispers in a raspy voice, as if he's just woken up from a thousand-year nap. I squeeze my eyes shut and will him to go away with every fiber of my being.

"Leave me alone," I cry as tears leak from my eyes, run down my ears, and soak my bedsheets.

He calls to me again, and a burst of heat erupts in front of me, so hot it singes my eyebrows. I cry out, opening my eyes to find his face close enough to touch. His pale skin smells of death and decay, and his long, pointed fingers uncurl so he can drag a sharp nail down my cheek.

"We've been waiting for you," he whispers sinisterly.

I shoot up in bed, both hands moving to protect my face as I cry out, panicked and breathless.

"What's wrong?" Dallas barrels into my room, tripping over a pile of dirty laundry in the middle of the floor. Sun shines through the window, blinding me as I search the room for *him*.

I could have sworn it was two in the morning mere seconds ago. How could it possibly be—I glance at the clock—eight-thirty?

"It happened again. He came back," I choke, fighting back tears as I bring my knees to my chest and bury my face between them. "He won't stop."

"Who?" Dallas asks, confused. Sitting behind me on the bed, he pulls me into him so I'm curled against his side. "Aspen, what are you talking about?"

"The man. The one from the other night. He came back."

"Who is he?"

"I don't know. H-he was in the room." I point to the open window, where a damp, morning breeze dances with the curtains.

"Someone was in here? Why didn't you scream?" Dallas holds me tighter as I sob.

"I did, but no one heard me," I whisper. He doesn't say anything more, just holds me until my tears dry. While I try to collect myself, a thought occurs to me. "Dal, did you sleep with the lamp on last night?"

He shifts so he can look at me. "Of course. Why would you ask that?"

"No reason." I shrug. It's clear he doesn't believe me, clear he thinks I've gone completely bonkers. I can't blame him, though. I'm not so sure I'm of sound mind right now, either.

I've had nightmares many times before, but they've never felt so real.

"Hey, what happened to your face?" Dallas asks, brushing a finger over my left cheek. The skin burns where he touched it, sending a jolt of discomfort through my body.

My stomach churns, and I feel like I might throw up at any second. "I—I don't know."

My lie isn't convincing, but thankfully, Mom's voice interrupts whatever Dallas might have said next.

"Aspen, honey, there's someone on the phone for you."

"Thanks, Mom!" I holler, trying to get a grasp on my shaking voice.

"Who's calling you?" Dallas asks, sounding surprised.

"My friend," I say, then clear my throat and wipe my fingers under my eyes. "She's giving me a tour of the town if you'd like to come."

"That's all right—don't think there's much more to it than what I've seen."

"You never know," I warn, and my thoughts wander to the Draven family and the uncharacteristically moody residents in town, not to mention my abnormal dreams. I purse my lips, considering the words more carefully as I repeat them. "You never know."

"Aspen, the phone!" Mom calls again.

"Tell Elaine I'll be ready in a minute," I holler, then gather my clothes to change in the bathroom. As I'm walking past the couch, prepared to go meet my new friend, Father beckons me to his side. That's odd enough in itself, let alone him being awake this early in the morning.

"I pulled out those files you wanted." He motions for me to

sit beside him. "I don't know what you're looking for, but I didn't find anything out of the ordinary."

My stomach sinks. I was hoping for something that might explain the terrifying man in my dreams. This was my only lead.

"Although..." he mumbles thoughtfully, and my hopes soar. "That family you asked me about, the Drovers?"

"Dravens," I correct him, easing down onto the edge of the couch cushion.

"Yes, well, you were right about one thing—they did reside here a lot. They rented the house off our ancestor. It says here..." His voice trails off as he pulls out a file with a heart crest on the front. Winding vines snake up and around the shape, an incredible match to my pendant. He flips through a couple of pages, searching for something. "Ah, yes. Here it is. The Draven family rented out the house once a month, usually on Fridays, sometimes on Saturdays, too."

"Do you think they've kept coming here all these years?" I ask, snatching the file.

"I highly doubt it." He shakes his head, picking up a bottle of... water? "These records go back two hundred years. This is one of many files I have up until your great, great, great, great-grandfather moved to the United States. I just find it hard to believe no one ever spoke of our relatives from London."

Father seems just as perplexed by the situation as I am. Maybe that's why he doesn't have his staple beer in hand. Or maybe it's just too early, even for him. Regardless, we've both spent the better part of our lives believing our family was Italian. Why would our ancestors destroy all traces of being here except for a few meaningless documents?

COME NIGHTFALL | 37

"Ambrose Draven," I murmur, reading off the name at the bottom of a renters' application. The signatures rotate between his and a man named Edgar Draven, though Ambrose was here significantly more. It looks like he actually lived here for a while toward the end of 1804, but after that, the paper trail goes cold. I can't believe my ancestor kept such impeccable records, and then just up and abandoned the place as if it never existed.

A square newspaper clipping peeks out from the stack of papers my father's shuffling through. I pinch it between my fingers, reading the headline. The words are slightly smudged, as though a thumb smeared them before the ink had dried.

Town Local Goes Mad in Covert Lodge
Last evening, the body of Ambrose Draven was found by local teens hunting in the woods, where it is believed he went insane and slashed his wrists and throat.

It was unbeknownst to many that Draven was still in town after his violent outburst toward Camden Vonner on November 2. Officials are calling his death a psychiatric breakdown...

The article goes on to describe his death in more detail, and it suddenly makes sense why this house has such an awful reputation. A man went crazy and died in this very house. No, not just died, he killed himself with no rhyme or reason—that anyone knew of, at least. I scan the article for an image of him, but I'm disappointed to find there are none.

In fact, besides what I've just learned, there's nothing else useful in the stack of papers. Still, I can't shake the feeling that there's more to the Draven family, more to my house, than I could ever begin to imagine.

Maybe there's more to this quaint little town than I'd anticipated.

CHAPTER 5

"Took you long enough." Elaine bounces down the front steps, and I feel the urge to warn her they could snap at any moment. My footsteps follow her path, much more delicately, as she leads the way through my yard and to the crumbling brick road. "Oliver can't make it, so it's just going to be us."

"So, where are you taking me?" I ask, thinking about what my brother said—there isn't much to see around here. The main attractions are the town square, and as creepy as it may be, my house. So unless she plans to take me hiking through the woods, I've witnessed everything there is to see in this small town.

Still, it's weird to me that there are so many stories told about the old, haunted house at the end of Cove Street, and yet not a single one is the same. They range from crazy ax-murdering families who liked to break into occupied homes in the night and ax them to death, to children who could see the dead and talk to animals. There is one common thread, though, between each of the disturbingly detailed stories: every one of them is mad. Every one of the stories has a psychotic element to it.

"I'm going to show you everything there is to see in this hick-ville town, and I will convince you that it's more than fruit carts and creepy beer distributors." Her burnt ponytail swishes in front of me, the pep in her step too much for me to handle at nine in the morning.

"How did you...?"

"I saw you walk out of there yesterday. Ted can be a bit creepy, but he means well and he's very generous. He's also the town's only handyman, so if anything ever breaks in your house, it's helpful to be on his good side."

I laugh softly. Everything in my house is broken, so I'm going to need to do some major sucking up. I don't tell Elaine this, though—I'd rather not advertise that the doors are dangling from their rusted hinges, and that, whenever it storms, the rainwater seeps through the roof.

As if reading my mind, she slows so I can catch up with her long legs. "Where did you live before this?"

Where did I live, or how did I live? Because those are two very different things. "Breckenridge, Colorado," I sigh, thinking back to better days. Better living conditions. Air conditioning.

"The Rocky Mountains?" I nod. "Holy shit, that explains your name. Don't get me wrong, we have some strange names here, but they're just the kind that are modernized or die off with time. Aspen is one I've never heard. Don't you have a brother?"

"Yeah, his name's Dallas, after the Dallas Peak. My parents were in love with the mountains even before they loved each other." I look down at my shoes, avoiding Elaine's gaze. There's no way I could tell her the truth, that my real name isn't Aspen Troy. That's only what I changed it to when we moved here. That Dallas isn't Dallas. My mom isn't Corrine, and my father isn't Anthony. We needed new names so we couldn't be tracked down and decided that the best way to honor our old lives would be to name ourselves after them… after all, our names are the closest we'll ever get to going home.

Dallas isn't just my older brother either, but my fraternal twin. We left that out when we crafted our new identities, knowing if anyone ever looked for us, 'twins' would be a red flag.

"That's so cool. I wish my name was something exotic, like Alaska. Ooh or Virginia!" She pauses. "Wait, no, that sounds like an old lady. Paris. That's more like it."

"Or London…" I offer, given it's where we currently reside.

She shrugs me off. "London would be so awkward. 'What's your name? Where are you from?' London, times two. Okay, I take back what I said about an exotic name. I just love how yours has meaning. There's a story there, and I love that. No stories come along with a name like mine."

I don't bother trying to make her feel better. She wouldn't be so jealous if she found out the wretched story behind the birth of my name.

A tall, bleached blonde girl with a deep navy shirt and dark jean shorts walks toward us. She carries a basket of fruit, which looks to be mostly strawberries and blueberries. She holds herself high, her radiant skin shadowed by the blowing trees above, but she looks about as miserable as can be. Her cheeks are hollowed, and her eyes dark as night. Looking up suddenly, she locks in on my gaze.

"Excuse me?"

I stare at her, all manners failing me completely. Lucky for me, she doesn't wait for recognition, she just keeps talking.

"You're new here, right? Aspen Troy? My mother sent me to bring you a welcome basket." She thrusts the basket into my arms and looks around awkwardly. "So, uh, welcome."

And then she turns and walks away. No introduction, no smile, just a cold greeting and some fresh-picked berries. "What the—"

"That was Gwen Griffith, dear friend of the Dravens."

Everything comes back to that one Godforsaken family.

"Are they all..."

"Rude?" she finishes for me, toeing her sandal into the loose gravel. "Not particularly. But when they sink their teeth into someone, they change. It's like, if the Dravens want to be your friend, you have to drop everything and everyone for them."

Elaine spits her words out like she's been waiting a long time to tell them to someone willing to listen. "You know, no one in this town believes me. But they're just scared."

"And you're not?" I counter, hoping it doesn't sound like I, too, don't believe her. She doesn't respond, so I continue pressing. "You sure know a lot about them."

If the Dravens like to keep themselves private, how does she know them well enough to have a personal vendetta?

We reach a clearing of trees at the end of the shortcut Dallas warned me not to walk alone. We've made it to town in half the time we would've had we followed the normal path. "My ex-whatever is one of them."

"A Draven?" I ask, astounded. I wouldn't have pegged dark, moody, and brooding as Elaine's type.

"No, no, he's not part of their family, but he is part of their... their cult, for lack of better words. It's not often they extend a hand to newcomers, but eventually they got Owen. He completely ghosted me. We were—" Elaine leans on the side of a tree, sliding down so her butt rests in the tall grass. "Owen and I were something special. I'd never really had an interest in the other boys in town before he moved here, and I haven't since."

"What happened?"

Elaine gnaws at her lip as her fingers twist the loose strands of hair that escaped from her ponytail. "The Dravens happened," she huffs, picking up a rock and chucking it at the nearest bush. "I really don't know. All I do know is he started hanging around with them, and I could feel the shift. When he was with me, his mind was always somewhere else. It wasn't the same. And then he was just gone. I've seen him around, but he acts like they do, pretending he doesn't even know me. Like he never knew me."

"Have you tried talking to him?" I ask.

Her dubious expression tells me all I need to know. Talking is out of the question. Punching and kicking, though? That seems to be quite the possibility for my new friend.

"Enough about me." She holds out her hand for me to take, and I pull her back to a standing position. She brushes off her shorts and moves toward town before I can even process our conversation. "Let's show you what our little town has to offer."

CHAPTER 6

The sunset is just barely brushing the horizon when we get back to town, and when we reach Elaine's house, she turns and hugs me tight. "Today was fun. It's nice to have another girl around."

I squeeze her back, happy to have a friend. "Well, thank you for taking a chance on the weird new girl."

She slaps my arm, laughing loudly. "You're not weird!"

I tilt my head, staring at her in disbelief.

"I'm serious! Just because you moved into the house rumored to drive people crazy doesn't make you weird!"

So she does know the true story... I wonder how many other people do?

Once we part, I walk swiftly back to my house, making it there in record time, and close the door. In need of a distraction, I seek out my brother, who's in the same position he's been in for the last week, bent over his work.

"Do you ever move?" I ask, announcing my presence before I scare him.

"I did today, actually. I painted." He smiles at me proudly.

Dallas hasn't painted since we left home, and it warms my heart to know he's found his passion for acrylics again.

"Let me see," I say and am surprised when he doesn't resist.

"It's not quite finished, but..." Dallas makes a grand show of pulling the white cloth from his canvas, revealing the stunning image of a man. He sits, posed on a wooden stool with a gray background. His expression is serious, with a hint of a smile playing on his lips as his deep black hair curls around his face. His thumb rests beneath his chin, showing off a large, tacky ring with tree branches swirling through the circular design.

"Dallas," I say, touching his arm lightly. "Who is that?"

He shrugs carelessly, removing my hand from his arm and rummaging through stacks of papers on the antique desk that had been left for the mice before we moved in. "I found a picture of him beneath a loose floorboard. Can you believe it? 1798, that has to be, what...?"

"Two hundred years ago," I breathe. Dallas flips over the image to read the writing on the back. "Ambrose Draven, 1798," I read aloud, my heart stopping. "Yeah, he went mad in this house. Committed suicide."

Dallas's eyes grow wide, glancing at his beautiful work of art with discomfort. "How do you know all of this?"

I bite my tongue, never taking my attention from the painting's empty, soulless eyes. "It's common knowledge in town," I lie, unwilling to tell him the full truth. "You know, I just remembered I left a basket of berries at Elaine's house. Some girl in town gave me them earlier today as a welcome. I'll be back soon."

At least this part is true. When we passed Elaine's house on the tour, she offered for me to leave the basket at her house.

Moving as fast as I can down the steps, I swing the front

door open, ignoring my parents' protests and questions. It's nine-thirty and I'm going on a walk in the dark in a strange town, but is it really any worse out there than it is in my own room at night? In my own head? This is all connected—my nightmares, the painting, this house—I just don't understand how, yet.

There has to be a reason Ambrose Draven is haunting me.

The second I saw his image on Dallas's canvas, I knew. I knew the man who was haunting me was the one who went mad in this house two hundred years ago. But why? Why me? Why not Dallas or Mom or Father? It doesn't make sense. Why am I the only one who can see him, the only one who has the nightmares?

The sound of a twig snapping makes me halt. My eyes search the area for anything out of the ordinary, but there's nothing but the low breezing wind and old moaning trees. Still, my paranoia doesn't subside as I make my way up the rest of the rickety path into the town square. It's completely vacant, just a few streetlights, which do nothing to hold back the darkness of night. My footsteps echo off the surrounding buildings, making it sound like I'm not the only one walking through this deserted part of town.

The wind picks up, and I have to hold my hair back so I can see what's in front of me. I've never seen weather this crazy or unpredictable in my life. Leaves blow in circles around me and the trees cry out in protest as the wind pushes them. Maybe I was wrong. Maybe worse things can happen to me out here.

The craziest thought occurs to me then—maybe the house was the only thing protecting me.

But that's insane. That old thing can't even shelter us from the rain, let alone protect me from dream demons or whatever the hell that thing is supposed to be. Plus, I'm not asleep right now, so Ambrose can't get to me... or at least I hope he can't.

The crunching of a heavy boot makes the air around me grow still, and I hold my breath, hoping that if I don't move, whatever is out there will go away. It's no mere coincidence that I've heard two noises, each from about the same distance behind me. I'm so stupid. There aren't any houses this far into town and all the shops are closed. I have nowhere to run. No one to hear me scream. No way out.

A shadowy figure steps out from the woods with a hat pulled low and what looks to be a crossbow in his hands. The streetlights help hide his face, but not his build—tall, strong. Deadly. He's looking straight at me and a part of me hopes there's someone else, that I'm not alone and it's not me he's staring at. Except one glance over my shoulder revokes that theory.

"Who are you?" I call, my voice shaking so badly it cracks. My legs go numb with fear as the blood flow stops cold, as does my beating heart. The man moves closer, but I still can't see his face under the shadow of his dark-brimmed hat. It's pure black with no designs, words, or anything remotely identifiable. "What do you want?" I try again, but there's still no response. I take a step backward and ram straight into an empty chair left out by one of the store owners.

I run.

I can't feel my feet hitting the gravel or the ragged breath escaping from my lips as I run faster than I've ever moved before. I risk looking back only to find he's directly behind me, close enough that he could lunge and tackle me to the ground if he wanted. So what is he waiting for?

I don't stick around to find out, continuing past town and

up a small dirt trail with overgrown trees and crickets so loud they might just drown out my pounding footsteps. The noise is, after all, the only way I know I'm still running. My entire body is dead from adrenaline and fear, every inch of me petrified. Why is this man chasing me? Why did he follow me? Is it possible he was waiting for me? Watching for me outside of our home?

The dirt path breaks into a clearing of sinking, muddy grass, still wet with puddles of rainwater. There's a thick layer of fog, shin-deep, that coats the entire area. I take advantage of its coverage and dive down, keeping my body as low as possible to the ground. I don't know how well it will cover me, but it gives me an advantage. I can hear the man squishing around through the mud as he searches for me, and I hold my breath as he gets closer and closer, until I can see the silhouette of him above me through the covering of fog.

He reaches out and I roll to the side, swinging my leg up and hitting his hand, sending the small bow flying through the air, too far away for him to retrieve. He's fast, though, grabbing my ankle and pulling. I scream as loud as I can while I use my elbows as balance and lift my other leg, bringing it down on his wrist as hard as I can. He flinches and his grip loosens, just long enough for me to free my leg from his grasp. My body flops to the ground and a pain shoots through my hip and down my leg. I grimace, and roll to the side, far enough to give me a moment's head start. I stand and brace myself for whatever comes next, trying my best to keep the weight off of my left hip, which is now throbbing in pain.

The man looks around, probably seeking his crossbow, but stops when he realizes it's too far to be of any use to him. He instead pulls out a long, sharp object, smoothly chiseled down to the handle with vines. It's hard to tell, but I'm almost positive it's made of wood. His fingers grip it so tight, his knuckles turn white. He looks angry, but even worse, he looks determined.

I've never known which is more fatal, someone with the utmost desire to kill, to get what they want, or someone fighting to survive. Which is more beneficial in a situation like this? Both desperate, both willing to do whatever it takes.

I know in my gut that we're both willing to kill in order to be the one who walks out of this alive, and I'm the one fighting for my life.

"What do you want?" I growl, my voice steadier than it had been before, laced with malice and hate. I've heard this voice only once before from myself. When a man tried to kill my family.

"I want you to die," he says, his voice deep and murderous. His chest heaves with every step he takes toward me, rising and falling with every ragged breath. I've worn him out. I'm agile and have more stamina—that gives me an advantage.

He swings the wooden knife and I narrowly avoid it, losing my balance as I step backward. He grabs my arm as I flail, and swings again, bashing me upside the head. His knife comes for my neck, and I block his attack with my hand, but he's too big, too strong, and my head is spinning.

"Please," I cry, tears welling in my eyes. "No." My voice comes out soft, meek, and I push against his wrist harder, even though I know there's no use in trying. I could never overpower a man this size. "No!" I cry out. He clasps my hand and twists it backward with deadly force. I feel every bone in my wrist shatter with his movement. He flings it aside as I scream, tears streaming down my face as I fight and twist and stomp on his feet. Anything to get away. I can't die here. I can't. What will my parents think? My brother? I've finally made a friend, it can't end like this.

Blood coats the back of my throat, raw from screaming my lungs out. The metallic taste finds its way to my tongue, the taste alone making me want to throw up.

"Don't," I cry out as he twists his shoulders back, ramming the knife as hard as he can into my chest. He raises his foot, stomping down on the side of my knee, as if to give me one final parting gift. My voice retches in agony, bloodcurdling screams escaping my lips. He stands over me, knife still in hand. He knows I'm dead. He knows he's killed me, why won't he just leave me alone? I try to shake my head, but it won't move. I'm paralyzed in place by the pain coursing through my body. And then the worst thought occurs to me: if he doesn't end it now, I might lay here until morning, suffering, just on the brink of death, and no one will know.

The man kneels over me, raising the knife above my chest again, but just as he's about to pierce my heart, he freezes, head jerking upward.

His eyes swiftly move across the tree-line, and he stands, backing away from me like I'm the plague. He growls, shooting one last look at his handiwork, and then takes off running back the way we came.

I try to turn, to stand, something, but I can't move. I can feel the blood seeping down my knee from where he crushed it, and my hand is useless as can be. My head, on the other hand, has sharp pains shooting through it, down my neck and to my hip, where I can feel nothing at all. The deep wound in my chest makes it so every breath I take feels like it might be the last. How could this have happened to me? Why me? What did that man get out of hurting me this way?

Closing my eyes, I think back to when I kicked the weapon from his hand. I never should have done that. I should have let him shoot me straight through the heart and end my life quickly, instead of in slow torment.

My voice doesn't work when I try to call out. Instead, I end up coughing up blood, the wound from my chest bleeding rapidly. With every breath I take, a sharp pain sings its way through me. I think there's a piece of bone splintered into my lungs.

Something moves to the right of me, and my heart drops. Did he come back to finish me off?

"P-please," I choke through the blood. "J-just k-kill me. Please."

A dark shadow presents itself above me. I prepare myself for the worst, and then I realize it can't get much worse than this. Only better. Only better if he kills me.

"Do it," I choke, blood oozing from my body onto the grass. It can't be much longer until I bleed out.

A hand strokes my cheek, guiding its way down my jawline and to my chin as the pain increases. The hand pushes the sticky hair from my forehead, and I open my eyes, but can't see much of anything. Just a blurred face and midnight hair that matches the night sky. His fingers linger on my forehead, his eyes seeming to contemplate something. With my good hand, I latch on to his wrist, which seems to scare him because he flinches and shifts backward slightly. I don't let go, gripping on to him with all my might.

"Kill me. P-please." I release my grip, all the strength leaving my body at once. I try to say it again, but nothing comes out but the sound of blood gurgling in my throat.

His head tilts, and he must make his decision then, because he places both hands on my cheeks, and whispers something I don't hear with all of the blood swimming in my ears.

"You can't," someone beyond us says. My eyes grow wide at the sound of another voice, all my fear rushing back to the surface. "You know what will happen."

The boy says nothing, just continues to stare at me with an intense glare. He lowers himself to a sitting position and removes the hair from my neck carefully, but I still flinch in pain. There isn't a part of me that doesn't hurt.

He shields his face from my view as he bends his own neck toward mine. "You will be okay."

His words ricochet off my skull, soaking into my brain like a cure. His hot breath coats my neck as I feel the sharp pinch of something piercing my skin. A gasp escapes my throat as my head tingles and my heart goes still, numbness coursing its way through my veins. I can no longer feel pain, just an intoxicating warmth in my blood, drawing me to a better place. I stop trying to hold on, allowing my eyelids to flutter closed so the world can take me away.

CHAPTER 7

here's a blissful place between life and death, where everything is nothing, and nothing is everything. I'm not living anymore, but I'm not dead because death would mean emptiness and that's not what I feel. It's warm and daring and intoxicating to the point of insanity. This is the place I want to be, the kind of experience people take drugs to feel. I can't see, but there's a light beckoning me toward it, pulling me closer and closer until I'm within its reach, and it bathes me with love and hope. The feeling of contentment is more than I've ever experienced in my lifetime. Ocean waves sound in my ears as they pull me out to sea, bathing me in happiness. The sound fills up my soul, keeping me safe in its arms until suddenly, it stops.

Dim light glows beyond me when my eyes open wide. I gasp deeply as oxygen fills my lungs, my chest heaving in relief. I brace myself for the wave of pain I expect to feel, but it never comes. I'm lying on a soft couch that cocoons around my body like a blanket, and yet somehow I feel like I'm soaring through the air.

Soft whispers capture my attention, though I cannot tell where they're coming from, just that they're not meant for my ears. One voice is harsh, rushed, and filled with angry concern, the other is more discerning, assured, and confident. I attempt to sit up, and while I feel small stabs of pain where my injuries are, it's still nothing like before. Not even close.

I must have cried out, because in the blink of an eye, a boy stands above me, concern lacing his expression.

"You're still hurt, you have to take it slow." He holds the back of my head, guiding it down to the comfort of the couch.

"Who are you?" I ask, slowly turning my head to the side so I can see him better. I squint, recognizing the boy sitting before me. "You saved my life," I stammer, my voice sounding groggy and rough.

I'm not sure how he did it, but I'm alive because of him, I know that much. He continues to stare at me, unblinking, perplexed, and I start to worry he's less of a savior and more of my captor. He must sense my unease because he finally blinks, dropping his eyes to the floor.

"My name is Miles," he says. "You're, uh, new around here."

I nod my head, or at least try to, and wince in pain. He snatches a pillow from a chair nearby and stands so he can lift me without incident. He pulls me upward slowly and maneuvers the large, maroon pillow behind my back. When he's finished, he returns to his seat on a nicely finished coffee table with deep caramel wood that reminds me of the one we had back home.

"How am I alive?"

Memories of last night return in fragments.

The curtains are drawn on the far wall, but they're so thick I can't tell if it's day or night. How long have I been here?

Billions of questions run rampant in my head, but I withhold most of them, knowing I'll receive answers in due time.

"You're not," a disembodied voice says sweetly, contempt wormed into her tone. I imagine this is the other voice I heard last night. The other person at the scene.

"Vanesa," Miles warns, closing his eyes as if he's the one in pain. "You're not dead."

Heels click behind the couch and a thin figure takes the chair slightly behind me. I find it unnerving that I can't see her face. "I mean, technically she is."

Scanning the room, I take in every detail, the perfectly sculpted antler chandelier, champagne-colored walls, rosewood floors, and still, my eyes roam back to the thick, black curtains trailing from the rod on the ceiling, draping down to the wooded floors. A rose-colored carpet sits beneath the coffee table, adding some cushion to the hard floors.

Miles rests his hand on my arm, and I jump, a whimper escaping my lips. It takes everything in me not to cry, and I mean everything. "It's complicated."

Miles looks at me with an aching expression, regarding me cautiously. His porcelain skin highlights his cheekbones and golden eyes. When he realizes his words aren't easing my fears, he squeezes my wrist tighter, and it's not until now that I realize it is the arm the man shattered. But Miles's tight grip is painless. How is that even possible? Panic rises in my chest. What if last night was another dream? Could I have dreamt up something so terrifyingly real?

Miles glances at his hand on my arm and releases me, averting his eyes to the side. "You are alive, that's all you need to worry about."

"Can I go home?" I whisper, tears filling my eyes.

"Yes," he assures me, but somehow, I get the impression that whatever is going on hurts him more than it hurts me.

Vanesa stands and I get a good look at her for the first time. Her pin-straight hair runs the full length of her back, brushing the outline of her petite, curvy hips. She grabs Miles with extreme force, pulling him aside.

"Do you think that's smart? Without telling her everything?" she accuses, a razor's edge to her tone.

He sighs, running a hand down his face. "She needs time." He turns to walk away from her, but she grabs him by the arm again, searching for something in his face. "Stay here. Do not tell anyone, Vanesa. Not until we have some answers."

"Our family deserves to know," she says, releasing his arm and spreading her own widely. The movement causes her sleek leather jack to open up, revealing a purple heart pendant with branches covering the surface. It's an exact replica of the one I'm wearing, the only difference being the color.

It's not completely unfathomable that I found a necklace similar to hers at the place their ancestor used to live. Even still, an unsettling feeling overcomes me, and the longer I think of all the coincidences recently, the more I just want to leave this place and never look back.

"No. Not if it's going to put a human life in danger. The more who know, the more unsafe it is for her on her own. We can't just rip her from her family." His words don't help my unease any, and I find I'm fighting to get up, eager to get away.

Silence ensues them until Vanesa lets out an unsatisfied growl, clicking out of the room with purpose. She leaves with one final statement that makes me feel more nauseas than I already am. "You can't protect her forever."

Miles winces subtly, his stoic expression hardly changing. "I apologize for her behavior. My family has never been one to open arms to newcomers, at least, not easily."

"I'm a newcomer?" I question, a mixture of emotions filling my chest. I'm not sure if I want to cry, scream, or run as fast as I can. After everything Elaine told me about Owen, I'm not so sure I want to be a newcomer. I'm not sure I want anything to do with this family... except I'm alive, and my curiosity gets the better of my apprehension. "What did you do to me?"

He doesn't say a word, just scoops me up in his arms like I weigh nothing.

"Does that hurt?" he asks, his eyes boring into mine. I try, but fail to read them, as if they could give me the answers I'm searching for.

When I shake my head, no, he reaches down to pick up a bag of... clothes? They look to be covered in mud and—

A gag escapes my lips and I have to look away before I vomit. Blood. My blood. There's so much of it. I hadn't even noticed that the clothes hanging loosely from my body are not my own. They've been replaced with a baggy black t-shirt and gray sweatpants, which I can easily assume aren't Vanesa's. I'm not sure she'd own anything that isn't black, leather, or skin-tight.

Miles tucks the handles of the grocery bag under the waistband of his jeans, all the while managing not to drop me. I silently thank him for getting the bag out of my sight.

"Who was that man?" I ask, not expecting him to answer since he hasn't given me any other explanations.

"He was a hunter. He wanted my family, not you."

"I don't understand," I say softly. My head can no longer

support itself, so I allow it to collapse onto his shoulder, into the crook of his neck.

"Your necklace. Where did you find it?" his tone is short and a little agitated. It doesn't seem like rescuing dying girls is something he enjoys doing in his free time.

I bite my lip, debating on whether or not to tell him the truth, or the half-truth I've been telling everyone else. "Well—"

"Don't lie," he interrupts, possessing a soft force in his voice. "I promise I'll believe you."

I'm not entirely sure that's true, but I take a chance anyway, telling him about my dreams. "I think Ambrose led me to it. I don't know. All I know is I was sleeping, but I thought I wasn't, and then I woke up in my bed with the necklace on."

"Ambrose was a dream walker," he says, making my ears perk up. Then he says, more to himself, "When he died, the magic that tied him to the house must have attached his spirit to it, allowing him to communicate with the living."

"What? You expect me to believe there's such a thing as dream walkers?" I gape up at him.

Miles shoves open a door with his shoulder, carrying me down two flights of steps. He looks around subtly, almost as if to ensure no one is watching us, before he goes any farther. He stops at a black truck, so covered in dirt and mud you can hardly tell it's black anymore.

A small smirk lines his lips, and he looks away as he changes the subject back to what I originally asked. "The necklace you're wearing is my family's crest. Every Draven-born daughter has one. When the hunter saw you wearing it, he assumed you were like me, so he attacked you. I'm so sorry. He must not have known what he was doing."

The more answers he gives me, the more questions I have

for him. He slides me into the front seat of his truck and closes the door softly. I barely have time to blink before he's hopping into the driver's seat. I look back toward the bed of the truck. How the hell did he get around so fast?

"So why does he want to attack your family?"

Miles clears his throat, cracking the window just a bit for some fresh air. "Because of what we are."

I'm about to ask what that is, when his truck bounces down the gravel, past an open area surrounded by a lining of trees. I can almost pinpoint exactly where it all went down. Where I almost—

"I could have died," I speak my thoughts out loud, the severity of the situation hitting me again. He could come back to finish the job.

"Aspen, I'm so sorry," he says, most likely thinking I blame him. "We do our best to keep them away but lately it just isn't good enough and—what's wrong?"

I rub at my eyes with my fingers, trying to rid them of the fogginess. Whenever I try to focus on something, my vision blurs and goes all wonky. "My eyes feel odd."

It's hard to tell, but I'm fairly sure Miles smirked. In what world is any of this amusing?

"You're wearing contacts?" he asks.

I nod—how could he possibly know that?

"Take them out," he instructs smugly, rolling down my window. "And throw them out of the window."

"Are you crazy?" I ask, scooting closer to the door. "I have them for a reason."

Miles takes his eyes off the road, resting them on me. I breathe in through the suffocating weight of his stare. "Trust me."

I've never trusted anyone in my life but my family, yet for some reason I find myself trusting Miles. I do as he says, removing my contacts and allowing the wind to whisk them away. I blink slowly, my eyes scanning out the window at the scene ahead. The weirdest part... I can actually see the world more clearly.

"Whoa," I breathe, astounded at how vivid everything is. The trees are so vibrant, their leaves the brightest shade of green I've ever seen in my life. There's so much color to the world I never noticed before. So much to appreciate. Something sweet floats through the window making me sigh in longing.

"A rosebush," Miles informs me, nodding his head toward a house where at least a dozen of them grow. I look over to him, and it's evident he can't take his eyes from me. He's intrigued. By what, I don't know, but something about the way my senses have opened up has him fascinated.

The sun is just sweeping across trees, barely above the horizon, and it makes the world seem so much more beautiful, more peaceful than ever before.

Miles stops a few blocks down from my house so we're shielded by the trees. Suddenly I find that I'm no longer afraid of the hunter man, and the dull throbbing aches through my body seem to have left me. I open my mouth to speak, only to realize Miles has already opened the truck door for me.

"That was... fast." I draw out my words, slightly afraid of putting weight on my knee even though it doesn't seem broken anymore.

Hell, maybe I am going insane.

"Careful." Miles takes my hand and helps me from the

truck. I slip at first, forced to latch on to his shoulder with my free hand. "You need to take it easy, you're still injured."

"Barely," I remind him, still holding on despite my feet being placed firmly on the ground. "Remind me again how that's possible?"

The smirk on his face leaves everything to the imagination. He's not going to tell me. I turn to walk away, but he grabs hold of my wrist, yanking me into him. "You can't tell anyone."

"I wasn't going to," I say softly, not feeling the need to remind him everyone would think I was crazy if I did. How am I supposed to convince anyone of what happened when I don't have a single clue myself? He releases my arm. Before I can walk away again, his fingers find the blonde locks of hair hanging in my eyes and sweeps them off to the side. His hand lingers for a moment before he steps away, heading back to his truck.

"Thank you." I speak so quickly it sounds forced. "Whatever you did, it saved my life."

"I hope so." He jumps into his truck, shifting it into reverse without bothering to turn around. I rotate in a slow circle, following his vehicle as far as I can see down the long path to town.

I could have sworn his eyes never left me.

CHAPTER 8

Smells of mildew and dirt flood my nose the second I walk through the front door. It bangs closed behind me, and I jump at how loud it sounds, vibrating throughout the entire house. But no one comes running. No one is waiting for me with prepared lectures on why I should call when I won't be home or how reckless it was of me to leave in the middle of the night.

My father is still asleep on the couch, and from the lack of creaking upstairs, Mom isn't awake yet, either. I guess neither of them were too concerned when I never came home. The clock in the kitchen tells me it's five-thirty, which means I have a little bit of time to sleep before the rest of the house gets up. Except I'm not the least bit tired. Sore, sure, but not tired. I feel a sense of radiance beneath my skin. Warm and exciting, the feeling stretches to my chest.

I tiptoe as softly as I can into my bedroom, removing my tennis shoes and climbing into my warm, secure bed. I may not be tired, but just lying down on my own mattress makes everything feel better, however uncomfortable it is. The blankets quickly grow hot from my body heat, wrapping me in a tight little burrito. I've never felt so safe. It only then occurs to me that I probably look like death...

Too soon for ironic jokes.

Reaching for my alarm clock, I tilt it until I find the perfect angle to see my reflection against the rising sun. It's hard to tell, but it looks like I have dried mud caked to my cheeks and all through my hair. There's a little red dot on my forehead which must be where the man hit me.

Simply thinking about him makes me want to vomit, though I probably couldn't, not with my stomach feeling so empty. It doesn't take me long to give up on rest and busy myself in the kitchen, reheating the pancakes Mom made for breakfast the other morning. I find the syrup in a small container in the fridge, and douse the sugary dough with it. The first bite is absolute heaven. I don't think I've ever appreciated a pancake more in my life. The chocolate chips melt on my tongue with each bite, and I savor the sweetness as much as possible before it turns soggy in my mouth.

"What did you do, get run over by a bus?"

A piece of pancake falls from my mouth and the fork I'm holding hits the ground. Dallas stands behind the couch, looking at me like I'm missing an eyeball. I stare at him, not fully decided on a cover story yet.

"I fell," I blurt, shrugging him off, and rinsing my fork in the sink so I can continue eating these heaven-sent pancakes.

"Jesus, how many times?" He gawks, taking a few steps closer. "And off of a cliff?"

"Don't be ridiculous," I sigh, finishing up the last of my breakfast. I find that I'm still hungry. "I took the shortcut in the woods and yes, yes, before you scold me, you told me not to. I just needed some fresh air."

"Did you hit your head?" His eyes scan my face, landing on the now purplish bruise at the top of my forehead.

"Yes, but it's just a scrape. See?" Like an idiot, I press on my wound. "Doesn't hurt."

Mother f—

"I promise, Dallas," I continue when he doesn't look sold. "I'm entirely fine."

"You promise."

"Yes. I do."

He still doesn't look convinced. "Well, go shower, you look disgusting."

"Gee, thanks." Setting my plate in the sink, I waltz past my brother into our joined rooms where I grab a change of clothes and a comb. I turn and find Dallas is still watching me with unease. "What?"

"You're… peppier," he remarks, earning a disgusted look from me. "And whose clothes are those? You left in your jean shorts and that peach tank top last night."

"They got dirty when I fell, I had to change."

"Into whose clothes, Aspen? The chipmunks you ran into on your walk home?"

I tilt my head thoughtfully. "As a matter of fact…"

"Aspen!" Dallas throws his hands in the air, exasperated.

"Okay, okay!" I reach my arms toward him to calm him before he wakes our parents. "I stopped at Elaine's and she lent me her friend Oliver's change of clothes."

"Oh."

"Forgot I had friends, didn't you?"

"Maybe." He winces. "But that doesn't change the fact that you're acting strange."

"A good night's sleep will do that to a girl." I pat him on the shoulder, then say honestly, "I don't know, I just feel... good. Is that so wrong?"

He smiles faintly. "I suppose not. I'm glad."

For some reason, I don't get the impression he is. Or maybe he's just sorry he can't shake the past long enough to feel good about anything.

"Is that a new cologne?" I ask, catching a whiff of something sweet and spicy radiating from him. I stretch my back in attempt to get a better sniff, leaning in closely to his neck. He shakes his head. "Hmm, well it smells different."

"So do you. Take a shower," he orders, then cuts me off by walking up the stairs to the study. Tilting my nose down, I smell Miles's shirt, and it smells amazing.

I take a quick shower, making sure to tend to my hair a little extra, then make an appearance for breakfast where Mom's making—thank Jesus, the Lord almighty—more pancakes.

"Save some for the rest of us, why don't you?" Father jokes, eyeing the six pancakes I have piled on my plate. "You know you won't eat them all."

I shrug, chowing down on the buttery goodness and drown them in a half bottle of syrup. My father and brother stare at me like I have two heads, so I decide, for the sake of my family, to sacrifice the last quarter of my pancake tower.

"You guys were right," I say shortly. "I'm full."

Dallas seems to relax a little, and Father seems slightly impressed that I ate more than my usual bowl of oatmeal or yogurt. Little does he know I ate the leftovers, too.

For the rest of the morning, I sit on the porch with Mom, drinking coffee and listening to the sounds of nature. How could I have not appreciated these things before? This place is so much more than a dump when you're outside with the world at your disposal.

Around a quarter after three, the phone rings. I answer it because the only time it ever rings is when Elaine calls. It seems as though I'm the only one in the Troy household who has branched into the outside world. The rest of my family members are acting like hobbits. Come to think of it, I don't think my parents have left one time since we got here, which is uncharacteristic for the both of them.

"Hello?"

"Look out your window," she orders.

"All right, why?" I switch to a wireless phone and run up the steps to the study because the view from my bedroom window is blocked by a tree.

"Three minutes and thirty-seven seconds ago, Miles. Freaking. Draven. Walked past my house."

My stomach does somersaults. "So?"

"So? What do you mean 'so?'" she screeches so loud I pull the phone from my ear. "Where the hell do you think he's going? Don't think I forgot about your mini staring contest the other day."

"You're insane," I accuse, laughing softly. She seems excited enough, but I worry his presence in my life will bother her. Not that he's even an established friend, but we're not necessarily strangers either. "I've got to go."

"Why?" she questions smugly. "Because he's outside?"

"Goodbye, Elaine," I singsong, hovering my thumb over the End button.

"He is! Oh my God I knew it, I knew—"

Miles doesn't even walk to the front door. Just stops dead in the middle of the road, looks up at the window and stares, leaving me to wonder how he knew I was up here to begin with.

After running down the steps faster than I should for someone who just got the crap beat out of her, I throw on a thin, gray hoodie and a pair of loose, black shorts, making sure the bruise on my neck is sufficiently covered—God-forbid Dallas has any more questions or theories.

I sneak out of the house, quiet as possible, and walk until I see him leaning against a large oak tree in my yard. He's changed into a light gray sweatshirt, thin enough for his muscles to show through the sleeves and chest. His black sweatpants hang low on his hips, covering over the top of his white and black sneakers. A roguish grin fights its way to his lips when he realizes I'm staring, and he turns his head to look out into the distance... though the only distance around here consists of tall, green trees.

"I want answers." My heart races in my chest as I near him, walking until we're standing side by side, looking up at the beautifully sculpted trees.

He regards me hesitantly, then says, "Is that why your heart is beating so fast? You don't want answers. You're afraid of them."

"I want to know what happened to me, and why you keep saying things like you can hear my heartbeat or how you knew I was in trouble in the first place. Your house isn't close enough for you to have heard me screaming."

He moves away from me as if doing so could deflect my questions. He settles against the small shed behind our house. I follow, crushing the tall grass with my feet until I'm standing directly in front of him. There's nowhere left for him to go. "What do you remember?"

"I remember you." I gradually take two steps toward him so I have to crane my neck to see his face. He inhales sharply, eyes penetrating me with a hunger I've never seen before. "Biting me. Telling me I was going to be okay. I remember believing you."

My feet carry me forward another step, and his back flattens to the shed. "I remember the worst pain I've ever felt in my life, and yet somehow, you made all of it go away. And now everything's weird. It's different, and I don't know what's wrong with me, but I also know I've never felt so liberated in my life."

We're face to face now, and he tilts his head down to meet my eyes, chest rising and falling as the electricity between us intensifies. I can feel the wind around us pick up, blowing through my hair from behind. Miles closes his eyes, inhaling, and I can see him at an internal war with himself. "Tell me so I can stop thinking I've gone completely insane."

"You think knowing will ease your fears?" he growls, low and deep. He's fighting me.

"I don't know," I reply honestly. "All I know is I feel... alive."

Miles removes the hair from my shoulders, exposing the bruise around the two small holes, diagonal from each other on my neck, just below the edge of my jawline. His hands snake tenderly around my waist as he tugs me into him. He leans down and brushes his lips over the mark, sending a wave of goose bumps down my spine. He doesn't release me, but instead, keeps me tight against him, his mouth so close to the mark I can practically feel the sharp pinch of his teeth.

"You have a choice."

"Of what?" I whisper hoarsely. My normal voice would have pierced the hushed woods like a siren, breaking the thick blanket of quiet that's fallen upon us.

"You don't have to be like me," he says softly, his breath warming my body. I take a long breath in, getting a mixture of the summer air and his intoxicating scent.

"Be like what?" I reiterate his words, sliding my hands up his stomach so they rest on his rock-solid chest. I flatten my palms against him, feeling his heartbeat vibrate through my body.

"You're the first person in over two hundred years," he leans away from my neck, gazing intensely into my eyes like he's looking for the world. "We haven't been able to turn anyone without them going insane. We've been cursed."

"Turn into what?" I ask him, grabbing a fistful of his shirt. "Tell me. Tell me I'm not crazy."

"I'm a vampire." His voice drops so low I can hardly hear it, but in that moment, it's like the wind sweeps me off of my feet, dangling me dangerously over the edge of a cliff. I can't decide whether or not I want to fall.

"And me?" I choke on the words, shaking my head slowly, trying to make sense of my world being turned upside down. "I'm not like you. But I'm not normal either."

"You're in transition," he tells me, my own fear is reflected in his eyes. "You would have died if I hadn't—" a pained look overtakes his face. "In 1804 my family was cursed by another clan."

"A clan of... vampires," I say the word slowly. It sounds strangely foreign on my tongue. "Ambrose is the reason your family is cursed?"

His lips form a bitter smile. "You're a fast learner."

"What did he do?"

"Ambrose didn't believe in killing humans for food or sport," he says this so casually it makes me blink. "None of us did. We believe if you feed on a human, it's done once, and then you wipe their memory, only taking enough to satisfy your hunger. But the other twelve clans enjoy it. They live for the hunt. Everything was fine until Ambrose made the decision to fight back against the others, to try and protect the human race. He was outnumbered. They were stronger, and they took his soul, cursing the rest of our clan so that every person we'd turn would be without a soul and would slowly go insane. We didn't know at first, and we had to kill every one of our newborns before they killed someone else. But we couldn't kill Ambrose, so we locked him away... and... you know how that ended."

Miles pauses to collect his thoughts. "And then one by one, throughout the years, the clans, and sometimes hunters, have been picking us off. And not only are we unable to turn anyone because they were scared of us building an army, but we can't use our powers on humans either. We can't feed because our compulsion drives them insane, and without it, they'd know of our existence. Even our blood, which can also be used to heal humans, drives the person insane."

"But I'm not insane?"

"Precisely."

"Why?"

"I have no idea." He bites his lip, eyes scanning my face. "No one has ever made it this long without becoming hysterical."

"You said I have a choice."

"Right now, you're in transition. It's a sort of limbo between life and death, human and vampire. You can choose to either die a human or to become like me. And to do that, you have to drain another human."

"And by drain, you mean, you mean suck them dry." I swallow the lump in my throat. I have to drink someone's blood until they're dead to survive. A life for a life. "How long do I have?"

He squeezes my waist and I suck in a breath at the aching pain from last night's injuries. He must realize what he's done, because he releases his grip, lightly holding me between his hands.

"You don't have to choose. As far as anyone knows, you can stay like this, live this way."

There has to be a catch. "It can't be that easy."

If my options are become a vampire or die as a human, I can't just stay human without consequences, that wouldn't make sense.

"Don't choose," he pleads. There's a desperation in his eyes I can't ignore. "You won't be able to live with yourself if you kill someone. You'll lose your last remaining piece of humanity."

"I could never kill anyone," I whisper, tears forming in my eyes. I can't make that choice. I can't have survived death just to die anyway, but the thought of taking a human life just so I can live...

"I know," he says, stroking my cheek. "Do you have any more earth-shattering questions for me?"

Shaking my head slowly, I tilt my gaze to the ground. "No."

I take a big gulp of air, trying my best to collect my thoughts and sort them in a row. I had my suspicions about Miles, and myself, but I'd never in a million years thought the decision to become a vampire would be this... awful. I can't help the tear that escapes, falling and landing in the tall grass at our feet.

Miles gently pushes up my chin with his thumb, and I suck in a breath, realizing how close we are. I finally release his shirt from between my sweaty fingers and smooth it across his chest.

"Sorry," I say meekly. He looks at me curiously, giving me an almost genuine smile for the first time, a hint of amusement dancing across his eyes.

"I just told you that you might have to choose between dying or killing someone else. I should be the one apologizing." He reaches to wipe another tear from my cheek, but I turn away so he can't see me cry.

"Why did you save me when you knew you'd have to kill me anyway?" I hadn't gone insane, but he wouldn't have been able to know that at the time, so why chance it?

He walks up beside me so our shoulders touch, but he doesn't look at me, respecting my unspoken need for privacy. "You weren't going to survive. By the time I could have gotten you to a hospital, even with my abilities, it would have been too late. You were too far gone for me to heal, so I guess I figured you would have a better chance of survival, even if you went insane."

"How am I still me, though, if what you said is true about the curse?"

"It's true," he assures me. "But I don't have the slightest clue. That's why I told Vanesa to hold off on informing our clan. If word gets out to the other families that we may have found a solution, they will never stop hunting you. They'll want you dead so the curse can never be broken."

Shivers crawl up my spine. "How lovely."

CHAPTER 9

*T*here's a moment in your life when you realize everything you thought was certain is a lie, and it's one of the hardest things in the world to go through.

I'm struggling to take everything I once believed in and throw it out the window because I've learned something new, something that proves all of these things I used to depend on are a sham to keep me in the dark.

Most people are kept in the dark, and I suppose a lot of them never have this moment. They're lucky, the ones who continue on their merry way down a path that is exactly what they envisioned and planned for. They never have to question their beliefs or their morals. Because what are morals when you find out there are so many other alternatives out there, circumstantial situations that can change everything? It's so irrevocably simple for everything that holds one fragile world together to fall apart and come together all at the same time.

"What are you thinking?" Miles rests his forearm on the windowsill of his truck, driving one-handed. I swear he hardly ever has to look at the road.

"How insane all of this is. How much my life is going to change." I pause momentarily before speaking the worries on my mind. "Are you sure it's such a good idea to tell your family? I mean, Vira hates me, I don't think Vanesa is a fan, and Gwen quite literally couldn't even look at me."

"Gwen is part of our clan, not my family."

"Aren't they the same?" I question, dumbly.

"No. My family is blood. The clan consists of the vampires we've turned, and on very rare occasions, those who have chosen to join us—like my brother, Lucas. He was turned by an Australian clan, but was too human for their... ways. So we accepted and trained him." Miles pauses for a moment, allowing yet another new piece of information to sink in, before he continues. "The clan basically follows our command. I'm only telling my siblings about you, though I suspect Vanesa has lost her patience and already done so. The others will stay in the dark for now."

Right. I feel so much better.

No. No, I don't.

The steering wheel turns down a dirt path, just a few rocks guiding the way, almost as if they wanted a driveway that they could get up, but that was deceiving enough to make others think is overgrown and leads nowhere.

Miles groans as he pulls up to what must be their house. It's not the same location from this morning, and I wonder if that's somewhere separate he lives for privacy.

His sisters are hovering on the porch, clearly waiting for our arrival.

"Just stay in the truck for a minute." He hops out and locks the doors behind him, which makes me anxious. Why does he feel the need to lock the doors in his own driveway?

Maybe so I don't run.

Or maybe because his sisters were mean before I found out they were bloodsucking vampires. Before they found out I could be the answer to their prayers... does this mean each of them have killed to become like they are?

"Where is she?" A short brunette with hair pulled into a half ponytail zooms toward Miles's truck at full speed. "Is it true? Where's the girl?"

If I remember correctly from what Elaine told me that day in town, her name is Danielle and she's the youngest of all the Draven children.

"Not until you've calmed down. She's not a lab rat, Dani." Miles puts his arm out to block her path and she pouts, sucking in an angry breath.

"You turned a human?" Vira remarks, sounding astounded. My stomach sinks at the sight of her, knowing if Vanesa didn't accept me, there's no way in hell Vira will. "So it's true. Vanesa hasn't lost her marbles."

"I told you I was telling the truth," she hisses, walking up next to her sister.

"Well forgive me, but it's been two hundred years. I was a little hesitant to believe we've actually solved world hunger." Vira steps around Miles, peering in the window at me. The moment our eyes meet, hers turn midnight black. I unlock my door and open it carefully, deciding it's not the best idea to hide out in the vehicle while they all look at me like a blood-bag in the window.

Vira whips around, raven hair blowing in the wind. "Her? The girl from the market? You turned *her?*" Her tone does nothing to reassure my faith in his family's acceptance abilities.

Danielle breathes in, closing her eyes, "Hmm... yeah, it's

her. You can smell the transition in her blood. Have you tasted it yet?"

"That's enough, girls," a voice echoes off of the brick walls, making all of them stop.

"Come on, Luke, we're just excited," Vira purrs, giving him a devilish grin.

"Go inside. All of you," he orders. Elliot comes up behind Lucas, and this gets them going. The girls move as he comes into view. Lucas is the only one of the Draven kids that sticks out. Unlike the lot of them, his hair is blonde like mine and Dallas's, but brighter and longer. The girls protest but make their way inside, no doubt walking slower than necessary to overhear our conversation.

"Thanks," Miles says, nodding at his brother.

"Don't thank me." He shakes his head incredulously. "I think you're a fool."

Elliot stands beside Lucas, and eyes me up and down. It takes everything in me not to shift my feet nervously.

"She's going to kill a human?" he questions doubtfully.

"She doesn't have to." Miles brings a fist down on the hood of his truck, making me grimace. Lucas nods along with him in agreement. At last, someone else understands the need to preserve humanity.

"That's never been done before," Elliot reminds him, which is news to me. Miles never actually said it had been done, but I assumed it had happened before at some point in history. I can't imagine my ancestor was the only one who kept immaculate records.

"Will I really die if I don't choose?" I ask, and both boys snap their attention back to me.

"This isn't *The Vampire Diaries*." Luke laughs. "You have

more than twenty-four hours to decide. But your blood is sweeter than the average human's and it won't be long until other vamps start seeking you out for a snack—not our clan, but radical vampires passing through. I've heard once you taste a transitioner, it's impossible to stop."

That's it. That's the catch. If I don't choose, I'll be at a higher risk, and will probably die in a much more violent way.

I blink twice, expecting him to elaborate, but he doesn't. "How long do I have?"

"The longest a transitioner has survived is approximately a year, but no one else has ever made it that long. They're either tracked down by the scent of their blood and killed, or they choose humanity over vampirism."

I raise my eyebrows. Does he really want me to ask what exactly it means to "choose humanity?"

Lucas sighs, eyeing Miles as if he's failed at the only task he was given—informing me. "When you choose humanity, you're required to perform a ritual sacrifice. Since you refuse to take a human life via blood transfusion, you must drain your own, giving your life-force to the clan you should have been born into."

None of this earth-shattering information seems to faze Elliot in the least bit, as he hardly lets his brother finish, interrupting him and pointing his finger at Miles before I have time to process a thing.

"Do you plan to just release her? The first vamp she sees will know you're her maker." Elliot wrinkles his nose in disgust, shifting his accusations to me and then back to Miles again. "I mean, I can practically smell him on you. And then they'll all come, and we'll have a war on our hands."

"Not if we protect her," Danielle's small voice pipes up from behind the two large boys.

"Danielle, go inside," Elliot orders. She stands her ground and I admire her a little more for it.

She heaves a heavy sigh and crosses her arms in defiance. "We could feed again. This could open a whole new world of possibilities for us."

"Yes, but only if she turns," the oldest argues, sucking in a breath. He's losing his patience.

"We've waited two centuries, Elliot. We can wait a tad longer for the poor girl to decide." Danielle stands strong, but I can hear her heartbeat spiraling out of control. She's not used to standing up to her brothers, but I'm thankful she is.

Besides Miles, it doesn't seem as though any of them are thrilled with this new development, but Danielle is sticking her neck out for me even though we've just met. It's nice to have someone else treat me like a human being and not an obstacle in their way.

"Okay, then what? We put our own lives at risk to protect the girl who might never turn?" He starts to walk away, then stops, turning back to Miles. "Our lives were fine before. We don't need to break the curse, and we can't afford to start a war with the other clans. We're not strong enough."

In a flash, Elliot disappears into the house, slamming the door behind him. Danielle gives me a small smile, then disappears as well.

Lucas runs a hand through his hair, looking like he's not exactly sure what to say anymore. "We don't even know that she'll be able to turn. This could just be a fluke."

Miles grabs my arm, guiding me toward the truck, which is

exactly where I want to be right now: safe inside and away from his family. "It's not a fluke."

Lucas looks torn between wanting to help one brother and obeying the other. "You'll never convince them all to look after her."

"Then I will."

"You can't do it on your own." Lucas shakes his head, shuffling his feet in the gravel. "What are you going to do? Keep her locked away? Because that's the only way you're going to keep her in this state without being murdered, and we don't even know what happens after a year. Her body could start deteriorating. It's a losing battle, brother."

Miles closes the truck door after I'm tucked safely inside. I can hear his voice through the muffled glass as he turns to face his sibling, "Not if we win it."

The tires screech on the ground below as Miles shifts the truck into drive and we take off speeding down the long, winding path. Dirt kicks up behind us, and I wonder if he did that just to piss off his brother by suffocating him in a cloud of smoke.

My mind runs rampantly over this new information, and as much as I know I should be horrified and angry at him for withholding the truth, I'm not. I was meant to die last night. I should be dead, and as much as I wish my inevitable choice didn't lead to my demise, just knowing I have more time than I was meant to be given is enough for me.

We sit in silence, him not knowing what to say, and me not having anything to say. At first I think he's taking me the long way home, but after six right turns and the realization that we've passed the same building four times, I decide he's driving in circles.

He caves, breaking the silence first. "You were right. I shouldn't have taken you there."

"I mean, I wasn't gonna say it, but..." My voice trails off, eyes sliding out the passenger side window as we pass by one of the only other cars I've seen in town so far. Most people must not drive, though I can't say I blame them. When everything is this close together, there's no point in having car payments when the longest walk is fifteen minutes, and that's to the Draven house, which is farther than anyone dares to venture.

Applying slight pressure to a button on the door, my window rolls down slowly and I close my eyes, feeling the early evening breeze on my face and through my hair. Everything about nature today is astonishingly invigorating. I crave it, desiring the fresh feel of the elements throughout me.

"You can't get enough, can you?" My attention is stolen as I direct it at Miles, the other toxic-inducing thing on my mind.

Wind rustles his hair playfully as it rushes past me and onto him, blowing the long hair from his face and giving me a full view of his features. He wears a knowing expression.

"It's wonderful," I breathe, curious how unbearable blood lust becomes when I'm this obsessed with just the thought of nature, something I don't necessarily need to survive. "Does it always feel like this?"

He turns his attention to the road. "Only if you pay attention. Never take for granted the gifts you've been given. Most people would die for them."

"Where are we going?" I ask, still fixated on this new sensation.

He gives me a mischievous smile, sparking my long lost sense of adventure. "Nowhere."

I have the slightest suspicion that I would go nowhere with him any day.

When the truck pulls down a side road, there's a voice in my head that says any reasonable girl should be terrified, any normal girl would have run for the hills by now. But I am no normal girl. Unlike the average, the possibility of newness and danger excites me in ways it shouldn't. In bad ways that will one day get me in trouble... or maybe already has.

See, there's a reason I didn't have many friends back home, and it was that I was drawn to the darkness in people. Where they saw the light and potential in others, I saw what I like to think of as the truth most people keep buried beneath who they pretended to be. And I was enticed by it. My friends would cower at the sight of an unfamiliar face, afraid of the other layers that may lie beneath.

They feared the unknown. They didn't like change.

Meanwhile, it's all I ever wanted.

CHAPTER 10

*S*mall rays of sun cascade through an opening in the trees as Miles walks slightly ahead of me, leading us up a hill where a clearing lies at the mountaintop. As we near our destination, the path becomes rougher, trees seeming to grab at us from all angles, the rocks in the dirt becoming larger and easier to trip over. My heartbeat ramps up as I imagine all the possible ways I could fall and roll down the mountain. What would happen if I slipped?

Miles doesn't stop walking, but reaches his arm back toward me. It takes me a moment to realize he's extending his hand for me to take. He slows down enough for me to get closer, and I place my hand in his, allowing him to pull me along the slippery path. I've been so focused on not falling, I hadn't taken the time to notice how high up we are. The trees part to reveal a small rock that sticks out farther than the rest of them, surrounded by wildflowers and a view so breathtaking I find it hard to remove my eyes. Birds chirp happy tunes in the distance, fluttering around without a care in the world.

"I used to come here all the time when I was newly turned." Miles settles behind me. I can feel his warmth against my back and I lean into it. Not fully, but just enough. His hand never lets go of mine.

Designs of orange, red, and purple color the cloudless sky, more beautiful than any photograph or painting could do justice. Every fiber in my body is on edge.

"Was it easy?" My voice comes out thick and broken.

"Was what?" he inquires lowly, the sound vibrating from his chest through my sweatshirt, all the way down my spine.

My tongue feels thick in my mouth, and I'm forced to swallow before I can speak. "Taking a human life."

"It's too easy," he whispers, and the hairs on my arms stand up. His hand wanders across my stomach, sliding over the muscles formed from weeks of exercise and training before we moved here. I had to be prepared. I couldn't afford not to be next time, and yet, despite my efforts, it still wasn't enough to save me from the hunter.

"I had a brother," I say softly. The gentle breeze carries my words over the edge of the mountain. I'm not sure why, but knowing they disappear so quickly makes it all the easier to get them out. "He was twenty-four. Engaged to a beautiful and courageous woman I could only dream of being like one day. She loved our family no matter our dysfunctions and always made sure to do fun, girly things with me since Mom always worked."

I take a shaky breath in, willing the trembling in my fingers to go away. I haven't told anyone this story. My brother hasn't been discussed by my family since we left home. In fact, lately, I've had a hard time associating him as part of our family at all. "Derek loved soccer, claimed he could never give up the game, joined travel teams and got to see the world, but when he tore his ACL, things got tricky. He was doing good, taking it slow, b-but the doctor told him that there was a very slim chance he'd ever be able to play again. He—"

I wipe the tears from my face, hating that I'm crying for a man who took everything from my family. If my own brother is capable of doing something so heinous, what does that mean for the rest of the world? Derek was family. He was supposed to care about us, and he didn't.

There's a weight on my shoulder as Miles rests his chin there, pressing his cheek to mine. "He was devastated. There was nothing for him if there was no soccer, or so he told us. Told Rachel, his fiancée. The only thing that made him feel better w-were the prescription drugs his doctor prescribed. It was a small town, everyone knew everyone, so when my good, star-athlete brother said he needed more to ease the pain in his knee, they gave him more. Until they didn't and my brother started stealing them. He broke in to the pharmacy three times without being caught by the police. Rachel had figured it out, though, and when they were staying with us one weekend, I guess she'd planned to tell us and have an intervention, but when she tried to talk to him—"

Pain shoots across my chest in blinding colors. Tears flow from my eyes and I can't slow them down, can't make them stop. Feelings I abandoned long ago come flooding to the surface, no longer willing to bury themselves. "Derek got so angry. He was high off his ass, and h-he hit her, repeatedly. Dallas woke up to her screaming and saw our brother's silhouette standing over Rachel in the dark. But he hadn't been quiet enough, and Derek went after him next. I followed to see what the commotion was about, and Derek hit me in his blind rage. I'm not even sure he knew who I was when he did, but he wouldn't stop, and I couldn't fight him off. All he cared about was soccer, and when that was gone, it was drugs. My parents' bedroom was on the far side of the house, so my father couldn't hear. My mom got home from my aunt's house a little while later after returning a dress, and she found us lying on the floor.

"Rachel was on life support for a month before she woke up. The doctors say she might never walk again, that in fact, she probably won't. She doesn't blame any of us, but she also hasn't spoken to us since that night. I don't think she can. I don't think she has the strength to."

His arms squeeze me tight, and I wish it were enough to keep the pain I feel inside, but it's not. "Where is he now?"

"In jail." The image of my brother in a tacky jumpsuit flashes through my mind, his mugshot being the last time I'll ever see his face. "For attempted murder."

My parents burned all of his belongings, all of his pictures, even the ones with Dallas and me in them. Still, I managed to snag one of him from before, when he was happy. Because I never want to forget. Without that picture, the only piece of my brother I have left is his threatening phone call from jail saying my testimony helped, and that he would only have to spend two years in a correctional facility before being released, at which point he would come for our family for putting him there in the first place.

Our lawyer had persuaded me to testify. She said if we could prove the pharmacist was slipping my brother pills, then Derek was the victim of unintentional drug abuse. I made the mistake of making an emotional decision instead of letting him rot for his crimes. He got off easy because of me. Had I left things alone, we might still be safe.

"That's why you came here?" Miles asks, his thumb rubbing circles into the back of my hand. "To escape what your brother did?"

I nod, looking down and then turning into him. He releases my hand and focuses his attention on the tears on my cheeks, wiping them away. "We were shunned, blamed for being related to the man who hurt the town's sweetheart. None of them cared that he'd hurt us, too, that we'd essentially lost two of our own. The people in town, people I used to call my friends, harassed us. We couldn't go outside, I couldn't go anywhere alone. I was forced to finish senior year online. They threw bricks at our house, lit our cars on fire. Then when he was going through withdrawal, Derek threatened to come after us, so we changed our names, found the deed to this junker in some of my grandfather's possessions, and came here."

"What was your name before?" I notice suddenly that he hasn't once backed away from me or looked at me with the accusing eye most give when they realize who we are, what my brother had done. He hasn't questioned my sanity just because that of my brother's wasn't intact. He just listened to me, and understood the pain I felt—feel—every single day.

"Destiny." I laugh at the irony of that. Destiny is such a hopeful name, full of possibilities and purpose. I don't have any of those.

He smiles, his lips turning upward and forming little dimples on either side of his mouth.

"Destiny," he tests out the name, rolling it over his tongue. "It's fitting."

"It's not me," I assure him. "I left that girl back in Colorado." Truth be told, I left that girl behind long before the incident. I haven't been Destiny Wilson in a very long time, and I'm better off because of it. I hadn't liked the girl she was becoming. I felt myself changing, molding into the person everyone thought I should be so I'd fit in better. She'd lost every bit of herself that made her me.

Somehow, Miles seems to know exactly what I'm thinking, because just as I think I'm about to lose it, he pulls me to his chest, and wraps my arms around his waist. I try to fight against him. Seeking comfort has never been in my nature, especially when found in the arms of a stranger, but he refuses to release me. His hand finds the back of my head and his fingers thread through my hair, keeping me pressed firmly to his chest. "You can't forget part of who you are, Aspen. You must remember in order to move on."

"But I just want to forget."

"If only it were that easy."

The sun has mostly set when we decide to leave the serenity of the mountain top, meaning the trek back down will be a lot more challenging than it had been on the way up. Much to my liking, Miles has other ideas, scooping me in his arms, and moving faster than the speed of light back toward his parked vehicle.

He sets me inside, pushing my arms away when I try to buckle my own seatbelt, sliding me to the middle seat so I'll be closer to him. Then he does it for me. I curl my legs into a ball to conserve heat in the thinning temperature. The mountain air is much cooler at night than in town, and my bare legs have goose bumps covering every inch of them.

Within seconds, Miles is getting in the truck, his jerking weight making it shift on its wheels a little before he turns the ignition and shifts us into drive.

Tonight's admission has me feeling sick inside. I haven't revisited those memories since the moment they happened. I just kept pushing them down and out and away, hoping one day they'd eventually be gone, but they never were. They've never been far. Always right there in the back of my mind, ready to ruin any good thing that might come my way. It's nearly been a year, so I suppose it's natural to feel this way, though I wish I could stop caring about my brother and what he did. It's just so hard when that was the person he changed into, not the one he'd always been. Because now he's probably almost eight months clean, and hating himself more than I ever could. How could I when he helped raise me? He taught me to ride a bike and to swim. Those memories don't just vanish when a person decides to become someone else.

The only thing I can feel right now is the cool leather beneath me. I'm numb to everything else. I don't notice the night sky or the peacefulness the dark brings. I focus on my fear, because it seems to be the only thing keeping me anchored.

"What if I turn out like him?" I quiver at the thought of my worst fears becoming real. "What if blood becomes my drug and I hurt people? What if one kill is all it takes and I lose myself?"

A warm hand clamps down on my knee, giving it a squeeze. "You don't give yourself enough credit."

My eyes close, and I doze off to the sound of the low rumbling motor beneath me.

CHAPTER 11

I jolt awake to the feeling of someone shaking my shoulder. Blinking slowly, I open my eyes to find myself in complete darkness, the only light coming from the moon's glow. I sit up, rubbing my eyes groggily. "What time is it?"

"Ten-thirty," Miles whispers, tugging a piece of my hair as he twists it around his finger curiously. "I didn't want to wake you."

Shaking my head, I lean forward, searching the floor for my other flip-flop that must have fallen off while I was asleep. The poor things are completely destroyed from our hike up the mountain. Had I known we'd be going on an adventure, I would have worn better shoes.

"My brother is going to be in a tizzy if I'm not home soon, if he isn't already." Pausing, I meet his eyes with my own, searching their depths. "Would you want to come in, maybe?" I stutter, silently cursing myself for asking such a stupid question.

His thumb trails my jawline, exploring the curves of my face.

"I shouldn't," he says quietly, a pained expression conforms his features. "The fewer people who see us together, the safer you are. The safer they are, too."

"Right," I respond, my voice barely above a whisper. I close my eyes, collecting my thoughts before I head inside. "Thank you, for today." I slide away from him, opening up the door and jumping out.

For a moment, I pause, listening to the creaking crickets and rustling leaves. "For everything," I say through his open window, nodding slightly. I cringe inwardly at my impulse to thank him every time he drops me off.

I'm met with a stone-cold face the moment the front door opens. Dallas sits on the back of one of our chairs that's directly across from the doorway. I give him a head nod, then walk straight toward my room, which probably isn't the best idea. "Where have you been?"

"I was out," I say, uncommitted, pulling my hair into a high ponytail. Dallas never used to be this paranoid or controlling. I think discovering what Derek was capable of, someone we loved and admired all of our lives, really messed with his ability to trust in anything. Not just people, but outside events that can't be controlled, stopped, or changed. I cringe, thinking of the hunter and what he did to me. If Dallas found out, I don't think he'd ever be the same. Actually, I think finding out I'm a transitioning vampire would be an easier pill for him to swallow than the news that a man hunted and more or less killed me.

"Aspen, you've been gone all day. Mom and Father were worried. You never said where you were going."

I search his reflection in the mirror, focusing on worry lines that don't belong on a face so young.

"Well then, where are they?" I ask, sighing outwardly. "Why are you waiting up for me and not them?"

"Well—"

"Dallas," I cut him off, turning and resting a hand on my brother's shoulder. "Be honest. They didn't even notice I was gone, did they?"

"They would have!" he defends, throwing his hands up in frustration, "You know they would have—"

Before.

His silent words hang between us, thickening the already sticky air. "It is not your job to worry about me."

My poor brother looks unconvinced. "Then who else will?"

"You've got a point," I joke. Then for my own sanity's sake and for his, I add, "You do know if anything ever happens to me, no matter what, it's not your fault."

Dallas's mouth opens, his argument well prepared and ready to be presented. I speak again before he can. "It is not your responsibility, nor will it ever be, okay? We all make our choices, and I don't want to see you blaming yourself for me like you do our brother."

"We should have seen it sooner, Aspen. We should have known something was wrong. He's our brother, we could have—"

"Could have what?"

"I don't know!" he cries, dropping down on my bed, burying his face in his hands. "Done something! We could have done something to-to help him or stop him."

I sit down next to my brother, grabbing his face in my hands and forcing him to look at me. "Listen to me."

He turns away, refusing to meet my eyes until it's evident he has no other choice. "Listen to me. You want to know something? I hate him. I hate everything about what he did and who he became because the brother I thought I knew was stronger than that. I wouldn't have blamed him for the addiction or making some mistakes because of it, but I do blame him for his choice to hurt Rachel and to hurt us. That was not him and you can't blame yourself for who he became because he chose to be that person. At the end of the day, he did that to himself and nothing we could have done would have saved him. If anything, things might have ended worse for us if we'd tried."

"We could have saved him. One of us could have gotten through to him."

"Maybe. But at what cost? Our lives? It could be you or me paralyzed right now, but it's not and as much as I love Rachel and know she doesn't deserve that, I can't help but be thankful it wasn't you." A tear falls from my brother's eye, and I pull him into me, stroking his hair like I used to when we were kids. Like I did again when his night terrors started.

He pulls away, eyes searching for something in my face. "Then when are you going to stop blaming yourself?"

"I'm trying, Dal. Every day, I'm trying."

A soft knock raps on the front door and the hairs on the back of my neck stand up. I take a deep breath, reminding myself that I'm awake and this is not a dream. Ambrose can't get to me like this.

Though he did do some hypnotism thingy with our kitchen mirror... never mind that. It's worse in my dreams, at least.

Dallas follows behind me to the door, keeping a close eye

on me. I press my cheek against the thin crack, trying to get a good look at whoever is outside.

"It's me, now open up!" a voice snaps, and I jump back at the sound.

"Elaine?" I gasp, whipping it open. "What are you doing here? It's eleven o'clock."

I move aside so she can come in, then close and lock the door behind her.

"You forgot that berry basket at my house." She smiles sweetly, clearly having practiced her cover story. There's just one small snag...

"I thought you went for the berry basket last night? Where is it, by the way?" Dallas questions, looking a little confused.

"We got to talking and I forgot it a second time," I explain, my heartbeat racing in my chest. "Anyway, uh, Elaine and I will go to the study so you can have your room."

He protests, but I'm already dragging my friend up the stairs by the wrist. Mom is sleeping, so we carefully tiptoe across the parts of the floor that don't creak as loud as the rest. Once inside, I close the door, bringing Elaine to the far side of the room so no one can hear what we talk about. Surprisingly, Father was in the bed with Mom and not on the couch like he's been for the last month. I also haven't seen him drinking as much, which is odd, but good, I suppose. Maybe this is the first step to establishing some sort of normality.

"Okay, spill," she blurts, removing her sweater and shoes, making herself right at home on the old, dirty couch we picked up off the side of the road. I wrinkle my nose in disgust.

"What? Nothing happened."

She looks at me. "The fact that the first thing you said is 'nothing happened' means that something happened."

When I refuse to speak, she leans forward grabbing my hands. "Oh come on, my love life is incredibly boring, as is my normal life. You're the most exciting thing that's happened to me since Owen and we both know he shut me out after becoming friends with the Dravens…"

I'm not sure if she's truly scared of losing me or if this is a ploy to get into my deepest darkest thoughts. Either way, worrying she's afraid she'll lose me the way she lost him is enough to get me talking. "Elaine, you have nothing to worry about. The Dravens will never pull me away from you."

"You say that now, but they already have. You're spending all of your time with him and none of it with me." She averts her eyes, looking out the window into the night. "Sorry, I probably sound like a clingy ex, but I don't want to lose you or see you get hurt."

I have to forcibly keep my mouth from reminding her it's been one day. One full day of Miles Draven. That hardly counts as blowing her off. "You are my only friend here. I won't jeopardize that, and if it makes you feel better, the Draven family hates me." I sit back on the couch, resting my head on her shoulder.

"Not all of them," she says suggestively, and I laugh.

"No, I guess not all of them. You can't tell anyone about us, okay? It-it's complicated, but we need to remain a secret."

Much to my surprise, Elaine doesn't bat an eye at this, she just rests her head on top of mine, patting my cheek like you would a dog's. "I got you."

Not five seconds later, Elaine jumps onto a new topic per usual, and this one makes me nauseous. "So how old is your brother?"

"Ew, Elaine—"

"What? I'm just asking! Be glad I didn't ask what his body count is!"

"Okay, I've heard enough." Elaine breaks out in a giggle fit while I fight the rising vomit in my throat. "And we're twins, if you must know."

I realize a moment too late that I've slipped, though she doesn't seem to think anything of my admittance. Why would she when she doesn't know I'm not supposed to tell people, and here I am, having told two separate individuals in a matter of hours.

She goes to respond, but something else catches her attention.

Faint taps sound outside of the study window, and Elaine stands, squinting out into the light rainfall that started soon after she got here. "Um, Aspen? You might want to see this."

Rising from the couch, I walk quickly to the window. Thanks to my newly enhanced sight, I don't have to look hard to find the figure lying in the lawn, soaked to the bone and shivering. "What the hell?"

I rush from the room, tripping down the steps and into the rain. Thunder rumbles in the distance, warning me this is only the beginning. I slide through the wet grass, landing hard on my knees at Miles' side.

"What happened?" I pull his face into my hands, smoothing away the damp pieces of hair.

He opens his mouth to speak, but his words barely come out. Lightning strikes above, illuminating his body, but as far as I can tell there's nothing physically wrong with him.

"Hunter," he chokes out, sounding like he has lead in his lungs.

"Okay, let me get you inside and then I'll get your family."

He shakes his head no, but personally, I don't think he's in any position to argue right now.

I stand, grabbing him from under one arm. I notice Elaine standing beyond us, arms wrapped tight around her waist. "Do you need h—whoa. I guess not."

"Elaine, get the door," I order, but she's already ten steps ahead of me, propping the door open with a shoe and holding my quilt in her hands. Miles's head drops, too weak to support himself, and I struggle to get him up the stairs and through the door. Fortunately, Elaine is oddly good in crisis, and helps me lay him on the couch.

"We need to get him out of these clothes," she looks him up and down, her face in awe of seeing a Draven this close. "Does your brother have anything?"

I shake my head. "My brother stays out of this at all costs. I have his shirt and sweatpants from last night."

Elaine raises an eyebrow but doesn't say anything.

"It's not like that," I insist.

"Hey, what you do with your body is none of my business."

"Elaine!" I curse, frustrated, then decide defending my character can wait until Miles is safe and dry. "Close the curtains and lock the doors. Make sure the kitchen is closed up, too."

"You afraid the storm might blow them open?" she questions, doing as I say.

I bite my lip nervously. "Something like that."

Between the two of us, we manage to get Miles into warmer clothes, throwing them into the dryer for a quick cycle so he can warm up faster, then switch the warm clothes for the wet ones, running the machine.

Elaine and I tuck him in with my quilt and a bedsheet for

extra warmth. I sit at his waist, stroking the wet strands of hair sticking to his forehead.

"I'm sorry," he rasps, his mouth forming shapes as sound struggles to come out. "I had nowhere—"

"Hey, shh, don't exert yourself. I'm going to get help, okay? We'll figure this out." The blanket moves at my side, and I shift it so he can maneuver his hand out. He reaches for me, placing his palm against my cheek. I press my own hand to his and pull it to my lap. His fingers are icy cold, and it takes both of my hands to warm his one.

"They injected me." He turns his head to the right, exposing his neck for me to see. There's a small hole there, surrounded by red veiny lines, almost like a rash.

He tries to speak again, but struggles. I move his hand back under the blanket, but he refuses to let go as if every ounce of his remaining strength goes into holding on to me.

Elaine watches us with curiosity, clearly surprised at how close we've grown since yesterday, when I hardly knew him at all. It's peculiar to me as well, though knowing he saved my life has bonded us in a way I couldn't have predicted. Just as well, our circumstances are anything but ordinary.

"Do you have any idea how I could get in contact with his family?" I ask her, but her eyes are still lingering on our conjoined hands beneath the blanket. "I didn't sleep with him, Elaine!" I defend, exasperated.

"Right. I'm sorry. Uh, his family. I make a point of having everyone's phone number in town. Theirs was a little harder to track down, but at least Owen was good for something." She sets her phone on the table, grabbing a pen and piece of newspaper, scribbling down a set of numbers. "You can use my phone, but here, this is so you have it. I-I should probably get going and give you guys some space. I doubt he intended for anyone else to see him like this. I promise I won't say a word, it'll be like I was never here. Whatever you're into—"

She grabs her sweater and purse and stands quickly, looking uncomfortable.

"No, stay," I beg. "I don't want to be alone."

I also don't want whatever may be lurking outside to harm her when she leaves. Truth is, I don't know how far the hunters will go to get what they want. It's strange that it's the humans I'm fearing, and not the vampires, the very creatures that drink our blood and prey upon us for sport. At least they have tactics and reasoning behind what they do. The hunters, though, are reckless and don't care who they hurt. I'm exhibit A.

That man—hunter—tried to kill me because he feared I was a bloodsucker, when in actuality, he's the reason I'm in the process of becoming one.

"Hello?" Vira's sweet voice drips through the phone like honey.

I swallow, wishing I'd rehearsed what to say. "Vira, it's Aspen, listen—"

Click. I blink several times, jaw dropping in shock.

"What? What is it?" Elaine asks, moving to the coffee table so she's closer to the phone.

"The bitch just hung up on me."

CHAPTER 12

Thankfully, the second time I call the Draven household, Vanesa answers, and while she's not fond of me, at least she doesn't hang up at the mere sound of my voice.

She speaks in a low voice, muffled by the speaker pressed tightly to her ear. "What do you mean? Is he all right?"

"No, it's bad. He said they injected him or something. It's hard to tell, but I think he's been poisoned." I almost ask what can poison a vampire, but remember Elaine knows nothing and Vanesa won't take kindly to me telling her or asking how to harm her family.

"I'm on my way," she says, her normally cool tone sounding a bit shaky.

Before she hangs up, I can't help but warn her despite knowing she can take care of herself. So can Miles and look what happened. "Be careful, whatever attacked him might still be out there."

"I won't come alone," is all she says, leaving me to wonder who else she'll bring with her. If my brother hears too much commotion, he'll make an appearance, and I don't want that. I need Dallas to stay as far away from everything Draven as possible. He's been traumatized ever since Derek attacked us, and the idea of reintroducing him to trauma is unimaginable.

Not five minutes later, Vanesa and Vira are knocking on my front door. The two of them look like they've just taken a ride through a hurricane, doused in rainwater and wet leaves.

"Where is he?" Vanesa pushes past me, not even bothering to say hello. It surprises me when Vira lifts her brows at her own sister's boldness.

"Come in," I offer, and she nods skeptically, eyes tracing the water-stained beams supporting the roof. I wonder how long it's been since she and her family came here.

Vira scans the room, squinting her eyes and holding tightly to her small, rose purse. She walks past me, carefully placing one foot in front of the other. It must be unnerving being back in the place where your uncle was locked up and died.

"I don't like wooden houses," she asserts, making her way to the kitchen to continue her perimeter search. She does, of course, pause at the mirror to wipe away the eyeliner smudges from under her eyes. "It's unnerving being in a home where every part could be used to kill you." She pauses at our dinner table, rocking a crooked-standing chair back and forth. "Even your furniture is wood. How ironic. Your ancestors really knew what they were doing."

She laughs hollowly, tightening her arms around her thin waist. Can she really blame them? They hosted dinner parties for vampires, they would have been insane not to take precautions of some sort.

"Vira, what are you doing?" Vanesa beckons her sister to her side, where she sits examining Miles. His body lays still, and

I'm honestly not sure if he's at all aware of what's going on anymore.

"We need to get him home," Vira says, removing the blanket from him. "Grab his feet."

My heart rate picks up, and I find myself laying a hand on Vira's shoulder. "No."

She whips on me so fast I barely have time to blink before she has me by the throat, back pressed against the coffee table.

Throbbing pains shoot through my back. I hear the wood splinter, and I pray it doesn't break because I don't know how I could explain that to Mom and Father.

"I think you've severely underestimated who's in charge here, Aspen." Vira draws over my name with such bitter distaste. "You played your part. Now it's our job to save my brother, who, might I add, never used to spend time in this neck of the woods before you, so if this is anyone's fault, it's yours."

I maintain eye contact, never allowing my glare to stray from hers, and her confidence wavers just a bit as she eyes me with intrigue. I'm not fighting her, I'm not shaking with fear or begging for my life. Vira's not used to being denied what she wants. "Maybe not, but I'm part of this now whether you like it or not, and I very well could be the only one capable of saving your family."

Her thin fingers contract so that I can hardly breathe, let alone speak. Her eyes flash red as she bares her teeth, growling low and angry. "What are you saying?"

"I'm saying—" I take my fist and bring it down on the bone protruding from her inner wrist. It's not enough to hurt someone with her strength, but she didn't expect it and that gives me leverage. I stand fast and she steps toward me, intimidatingly. "—you won't kill me. You can't, and even if you could, there'd be hell to pay for it. So your threats? They don't scare me."

Vira grabs my throat again, lifting me just enough to get my blood pumping, when Vanesa chimes in. "Vira, enough."

"You insolent girl," she says menacingly.

Vanesa speaks more firmly this time, her eyes flicking to Elaine in concern. "Vira."

"What?"

"I don't like her either," she says, looking me up and down with her soulless eyes. "But she's right. We can't kill her."

Vira shrugs, releasing me. She turns away and I rub my fingers over the tender skin on my neck, taking deep, calming breaths. "Kill is a relative term, sister. We can still harm her."

Vanesa looks convinced enough, but she manages to control her bloodthirsty urge to attack me.

"Perhaps a discussion for another time." She licks her plum lips, eyeing my neck with intrigue. Miles said my blood is sweeter because I'm in transition, which means I'm the human equivalent of cocaine. If they bit me, would they be able to stop? "We need to do some research, look up the symptoms he's having, and cross-reference them with the poisons we have on file in the armory."

Vanesa reaches for the door handle when Vira rushes to her side, whispering in disbelief. "You're just going to leave him here? With her?"

"He's safe with me," I ensure her, though Vira looks unconvinced. Her attention shifts to Elaine, and she doesn't seem so satisfied with my promise.

Vanesa, however, is more concerned with fixing her brother than my questionable intentions. "Somehow, I don't doubt that. We'll be back soon whether we find something or not."

The two girls click down my front porch in their knee-high leather boots. I move to the window, scooting the curtains aside just enough to watch them glance around my yard, and then disappear at the speed of light down the cobblestone road. I don't think I'll ever get used to moving at that speed or being part of a world where vampires exist. I suppose I've adapted well thus far, but I don't think the severity of the situation has sunk in yet, and it's finally beginning to.

"What the hell was that?" Elaine breathes out in relief. "I knew I would never ever want to mess with their family, but I never imagined it went further than money and a cleaning guy to tidy up their messes and do their dirty work..." Elaine trails off, sinking down into the recliner and massaging at her temples.

"They're a bit much," I agree, reclaiming my spot on the couch at Miles's waist. He hasn't moved in over a half hour.

"Can I ask you something?" She bites her lip, looking at me unsurely. "Maybe I shouldn't, but why didn't you call the police? I know we only have them in neighboring towns, but we still don't have a-a cure or whatever, so it's not like this was time-sensitive. I just don't understand what they can do that trained professionals can't. I mean, what if he dies?"

"He won't," I assure her. "He's a lot stronger than you think."

She looks at Miles, studying his exterior as if unconvinced. "Maybe. What kind of person would do this, though? Poison someone?"

"I don't know." Suddenly, I regret asking her to stay even if it was for her own protection. She's seen too much, and it surprises me that Vira and Vanesa let her witness as much as she did. It also makes me a hypocrite. Letting Elaine stay puts her in the exact danger I want to keep my brother out of.

"Did he, did he say a hunter did this to him?" she questions, none of the pieces she has are fitting together, and if I know Elaine, she won't stop until she figures out how to make them fit. "What would a hunter be doing out in the woods at this hour anyway?"

"It's been a really long night, why don't you go crash in my bed and get some sleep," I suggest.

"Where will you sleep?" Her incredulous tone is not lost on me. She's not buying what I'm selling.

I rest my attention on the boy lying before me and feel a small pang in my chest. He brought me back from the dead and I can't begin to understand what's wrong with him. I feel useless.

Shrugging, I say honestly, "I won't."

CHAPTER 13

Despite my desperate attempt to stay awake and keep watch, I find my eyelids drooping every minute, lulling me in and out of sleep. I take deep breaths, slapping my cheeks a couple times to keep my attention on something other than my exhaustion. "Come on, Aspen, stay awake."

After a few minutes of contemplation, I decide I can no longer sit here in the makeshift bed I set up on the floor beside the couch. I rise, determined to walk the room until Vira and Vanesa get back. Then I can sleep. Although knowing they'll be watching over me while I'm vulnerable isn't the most comforting thought in the world. They'd probably kill me in my sleep.

Switching on the sink, I let the water run until it's too cold to bear, then splash it on my face, rubbing my eyes and drying off my hands and arms with a dishtowel. A wisp of wind claws down my back, and my hair blows faintly.

My eyes squint through the darkness, peering around for the source. I could have sworn Elaine checked all the windows and doors. It's an old house, so we often get drafts, but none this strong.

A glance out the kitchen window tells me the night is as still as death, no wind in sight. Weak light from the living room lamp illuminates the kitchen, which is mostly enclosed in darkness. I narrow my eyes at the dull reflection of my face as a warm heat makes the hairs on my neck stand up. I see his eyes through the window—no, not through the window. Behind me.

He laughs softly as I turn so we're face to face. He moves closer to me, his face closer to my neck than I'm comfortable with. He breathes in, his tongue trickling down my carotid and across my collarbone. I flinch, backing myself up against the sink as far as I can, but his hands find me as his rough tongue trails back up the way it came, stopping just below my ear.

I clench my jaw, breathing carefully so my voice doesn't shake. It doesn't work, though. I sound utterly terrified. "I know who you are."

His long fingers sweep aside the hair on my shoulder, and he moves so I can feel the cold clamp of his body against me.

"Hmm," he moans, continuing his pattern on the opposite side of my neck. When he reaches my ear this time, he tugs it with his teeth, voice coming out smoky. "And I know who you are," he singsongs, sucking on my lobe with force.

"You went mad here." I grab on to the edge of the sink, closing my eyes so I don't have to see him. The smell of death surrounds him like a plague, his clothes torn and left untended.

He growls low in his throat. "Because they made me that way."

Immediately, I regret speaking at all because he pulls away, and staring into his dank, bottomless eyes is so much worse. Luckily, or unluckily, his attention is drawn back to my pulsing veins, and his hands slide up my hips, all the way to my shoulders.

I want him off. I want him as far away from me as possible, but I can't seem to make myself move. I'm paralyzed in place by the fear he's bestowed upon me.

"Your blood is sweet," he coos, smiling rabidly. "The blood of a newborn always makes a vampire feel new again."

"Have you—" My chest heaves rapidly as my spine digs into the counter. I need to distract him. "Have you ever tasted it before?"

His tongue slides up my vein and across my throat with an easing pressure. His lips part further to reveal the forceful pressure of his teeth, just barely hard enough to pierce my skin. "Many times."

"Don't," I beg, though begging has never helped me before.

I feel droplets of blood trickle across my skin and his lips follow it affectionately, savoring the taste. This time he doesn't play around, thrusting my head to the side violently while pulling my hips against him and sinking his fangs into my neck. He growls greedily pulling at my hair, blood sputtering out of his mouth and gushing down my chest as he speaks.

"Wake up," he orders as I thrash and fight against him, feeling around for anything heavy enough to knock him away. "Wake up!"

CHAPTER 14

I gasp loudly, shooting up and banging my knee off the side of the coffee table. Damp tears coat my cheeks, stained with a wetness I try to rub raw with force.

"Do you always wake up so viciously?" Vanesa asks skeptically, uncrossing her legs and sinking back into the living room chair. When I say nothing, her face grows more concerned. "Are you all right?"

Ignoring her question, I find my neck and wince as my fingers touch the place where Ambrose bit me. It's sticky with dried blood.

"What the hell happened to you?" Vira stands up, looking at me in horror, then at her brother, knowing he couldn't have possibly touched me since he hasn't moved in hours. The light morning glow outside lets me know that it's at least six o'clock, meaning I've been asleep for about seven hours.

"Did you find the cure?" That's all I care about. Without Miles, I'm as good as dead if the Dravens decide they don't need me. And it's only with his help that I can figure out how to stop Ambrose from invading my head every night and leaving very real battle scars.

"No, we tried giving him a shot of something that should flush out his blood, but I don't think it did anything. Whatever this poison is, it's strong," Vanesa informs me as Vira backs away, distrust shining bright in her expression.

Something Ambrose said stays with me, and I find myself mulling it over in my head while the girls stare at me.

"I think I know what to do." I swallow, grabbing the knife I used last night to cut off his shirt. I take the sharp point and slice it across my wrist, deep enough for a puddle of blood to pool, spilling over my skin. I turn Miles's head and let a few drops seep onto his tongue through his slacked lips.

"What are you doing?" Vira screeches at the same time Vanesa yells, "You could make him worse!"

I ignore them both, allowing a few more drops to spill down my wrist.

"No," Miles grunts, trying to push me away but he's too weak. "I won't be able to st—" His words fall short, and he breathes raggedly, gagging violently against his dry throat. He doesn't have much more time. Sweat glistens across his upper lip, his skin cold and clammy with a sickly pale glow.

"Yes, you will. It's working, Miles, you have to drink." He struggles at first, but once his lips are against my wrist, he loses his will to fight. His mouth wraps around me as his teeth pierce the thin layer of skin. His hands find my arm and squeeze, sucking the life-force from me. Lucas's words ring in my ears as my legs go weak, and I fall onto the very person who might save and end my life. *I've heard once you taste a transitioner, it's impossible to stop.*

"I don't have much left," I strain, my vision blurring over. I don't think he hears me. "Miles."

He grips on tighter, unwilling to let go. My arm feels numb, but I manage to lift my free hand high enough to touch his face, feeling the sweat beads on the pads of my fingers. "Please."

Miles drops my arm like it's smoldering hot and sits up on the arm of the couch. The room swirls around me in vibrant colors, smearing together and dancing across my vision. Round circles of light from the ceiling grow and shrink as I blink my eyes in attempt to clear the fog. There's a ringing in my ears, so loud it's hard for me to make out what Miles is saying.

"I'm so sorry," he says darkly as I crumple to the floor. He bends, trembling as his voice rises in anger. "Why would you do that, you know I can't stop!"

He cradles my limp body in his arms, reminding me of the night we first met. The night I was brutally beaten to death. If it weren't for Miles, I never would have survived. I would be a nameless body buried in the dirt, while my family was left broken-hearted and forever wondering whether or not their daughter was out there somewhere alive or if she died long ago. So as far as I'm concerned, saving his life was worth a little blood loss. Miles not only saved me from death, he brought me back to life, literally and metaphorically. "I couldn't let you die."

"You should have. I refuse to have you putting yourself in danger to save me. I won't allow it." I can feel the anger radiating from his skin as he smooths back the hair stuck to my dry lips.

"You don't get a say," I mumble, my head feeling fuzzier with each passing second.

"Why isn't she getting better?" He looks up at his sisters,

who are more than content with standing by while I suffer. "She should be healing herself, I didn't take that much."

"Maybe it has something to do with what happened to her neck?" Vira suggests, squatting down and pulling my hair aside roughly. She lets out a bitter sigh, as if she's not sure why exactly she's helping instead of finishing me off. "It was like that when she woke up."

"Ambrose," I choke, trying to swallow against the sandpaper in my throat. "I think he was trying to tell me how to save you."

"Our dead uncle, Ambrose?" Vanesa's arms cross as her interest piques. "How the hell do you even know who he is?"

I shake my head, the knowing is irrelevant. "When I sleep." I swallow hard, once again trying to fight against my extraordinarily dry throat. "He comes to me when I sleep."

"Vira, she needs your blood." Miles grabs her wrist and sinks his teeth into it. She yanks her hand back holding it close to her body.

Her eyes grow wide in anger, appalled at her brother's invasiveness. "She's your blood whore, you do it!"

He snatches her wrist again, which has already healed itself, but this time he doesn't force her into anything. "Vira, there could still be poison in my blood, I can't risk killing her. We don't know what it could do to a human."

"Possibly nothing." Vanesa shrugs unapologetically.

"Possibly. But I can't take that risk."

Vira grinds her teeth, eyes singing with hatred. "Fine. But I'm putting it in a cup. I'm not letting her grubby lips anywhere near my skin, I'd probably get a rash."

Miles closes his eyes, holding in a deep breath. "Fine," he grits as she takes her time searching for a cup in my kitchen. I try to tell her where they are, but her convenient super hearing doesn't receive the message. She takes the same knife I used and cuts it across her palm, squeezing her hand so the blood comes out in a short stream before the wound seals.

"That should be enough," she says quietly, handing Miles the cup so he can feed me. The warm liquid skates across my tongue, tasting bitter as I imagined someone like Vira's blood would be, but the second it hits my throat I can feel my entire body tingling in excitement, vibrating and bubbling smoothly over all of the broken skin.

I watch in amazement as the holes on my wrist close effortlessly, healing like magic, as if nothing was ever there.

"Thank you," I say, able to sit up a little more now. She doesn't look particularly happy about what she's done. In fact, she looks like, if she could, she'd suck her blood right back out of my system and then some.

"Aspen, I didn't realize you were having a sleepover."

All heads in the room turn to my mom and father, standing at the base of the stairs. Judging by their pleasant expressions, they have no idea what's just happened in their living room. Miles moves backward, putting necessary space between us.

"Who are your friends?"

"Leaving," Vira mumbles, but both Vanesa and Miles stop her.

"This is Vira, Vanesa, and Miles," I introduce, unwilling to give their last names after how many questions I've asked my father about them and their intertwining history with our house. The last thing I want is for him to stumble upon their names in an old file. "Elaine is asleep in my room."

"No, she's not." Dallas appears, mouth full of toothpaste. He removes the toothbrush from his tongue, gesturing behind him to my room. "She left a few minutes ago."

"What?" Vira gapes, probably thinking what the rest of us are—she saw something she shouldn't have.

I clear my throat, standing from the floor and dusting off my shirt, while my thumbs wipe around my lips, making sure to get deep in the corners. "I, uh, didn't see her walk out."

Dallas shakes his head, his gaze shifting toward Vanesa, who is still as a statue. "She climbed through the window. Said she didn't want to wake anybody up."

"We were awake," Vira says stoically.

"Won't you stay for breakfast?" Mom offers, extending her arms toward the breakfast table. "We have leftover pancakes and I was about to get a head start on some BLTs."

"Raincheck," Vanesa says, sweetly, showing more charm toward my mom than I thought she'd be capable of. "We should be getting home."

The girls make their way to the door, turning back to look at Miles.

"I'm going to stick around," he states, meeting my stare. "So long as that's okay?" he questions, looking at me deeply. My teeth gnaw on my bottom lip nervously before I nod my head with a forced smile.

"I'll talk to Elaine later." I give them a meaningful stare so they understand I don't want them going to her home and threatening her. She's probably scared out of her mind as it is without them getting involved. The sisters leave without another word.

I clean up the blankets and pillows before anyone notices there aren't enough for four people, and let my mind wander to Elaine.

Miles pulled me aside and informed me that they won't hurt her for finding out, but that we do need to see how much she knows and what we should do about it, considering their compulsion drives people insane. Mine might be the only one that doesn't, and I'm not sure I want to turn. And every day, my clock is ticking. If another vampire takes me first, I'll die before I get the chance to decide.

"Breakfast is ready," someone calls from the kitchen.

I look over at Miles, who has been watching me clean up, and lower my voice a few octaves, peeking occasionally at the kitchen to make sure no one overhears. "Do you even... eat?"

He smirks, rubbing his hand down his face. "Haven't you noticed a difference when you eat? More flavor? It's like that times ten for us. Sure, we need blood to survive, but we still eat food to satisfy other cravings." He stands, pulling me from folding this blanket for the fourth time because it's still crooked. "For example," he says quietly, pulling me to him. "The bacon on the stove right now, smells just about as good as your blood."

"Are you saying I smell like a pig?" I taunt him, rubbing my thumb across a quickly fading bruise on his cheekbone.

His hands find my waist, and he leans so close I can feel his breath.

"Aspen?" Dallas calls, walking from the kitchen. He stops when he sees us, and Miles backs away grudgingly. "Come eat," he says, eyeing Miles with suspicion.

When my brother's gone, Miles remarks regrettably, "He doesn't like me."

My hair swishes back and forth as I look away, disagreeing. "I don't know."

Dallas has never been the type to flash judge someone, so

I'm not sure why he seems to dislike Miles. It could be because he's never seen me with a guy at all, let alone standing that close to one, but who knows.

I think this town is making all of us a little worse for wear.

CHAPTER 15

*B*reakfast is most definitely not the most important meal of the day when you're a vampire, and I'm not sure why, but this is the thought that continuously runs through my mind the whole time we eat. Meanwhile, my brother drills Miles with question after question about where he grew up, why he doesn't attend school here, what type of hair gel he uses... basically he interrogates him about everything under the sun. Miles answers them in stride, though, and mostly embarrasses my brother by being a model citizen and saying nothing to implicate himself. This isn't his first time dodging nosy humans, that is for sure.

When the pancakes are all gone and the bacon sits cold on the plate, my mom gets busy putting everything away and I offer to walk Miles out. But when we get outside, we realize Vira and Vanesa must have driven his truck back to the Manor since he pauses in the yard, looking into the distance, and shakes his head.

I watch him, studying his movements, fluid and sure, imagining how anyone could be so confident in their next step when I'm avidly praying mine doesn't falter and knock me on my face. "So..."

"So?" He laughs, a knowing look in his expression. With a vampire, you'd think there would always be something to talk about, yet I find myself struggling to make simple conversation.

I finger my shorts uncertainly, moving the fabric so it stretches away from my thighs. "What actually happened last night?"

He breathes out heavily, resting against what must be his favorite tree in our yard. "The hunter... he lured me out. He must have known I'd recognize his smell from—"

Miles stops abruptly, a dark shadow falling over his face as his chin drops. The clouds do nothing to shield us from the heat, and we're left baking in yet another hot summer day.

"From?" I prod, suddenly tired of all the unanswered questions nagging at my mind.

"My sister." He adjusts the sleeves of his black shirt and looks into the trees as if they hold the answers to all the questions he has. I study his posture, sure and confident, yet still relaxed despite practically coming back from the dead not long ago. The cloudy sky parts and an orange glimmer of sunlight catches on his jawline, enhancing the clench he's using to grind his teeth. Whatever he's about to say, isn't coming out willingly. "She died about a year ago. In your house."

My poor little shit shack at the end of Cove Street has fallen victim to two murders? That must be some seriously awful karma.

My stomach churns, filling me with nausea. If we're living in the smack dab middle of Murder Manor then I'd sure as hell rather get out now than later. It's like my broken-down home is an allure for the peculiar.

"I didn't realize you had another sister."

He doesn't seem at all surprised at my lack of awareness, so I assume her death either isn't common knowledge or was kept very under wraps. They're one and the same, I suppose. Though I imagine it must be hard to keep your private life from everyone around you. I mean, people must get curious at times, especially when a recognized member of a family like the Dravens disappears.

"Her name was Emile... she was killed by a hunter. She had to have been the most kind-hearted one of us all, even more so than Danielle. But she wasn't naive by any means. The hunter had been stalking her, taunting her, sending her letters, leaving notes in her locker at school... Emile wasn't like the rest of us, she had human friends and—" He pauses to collect his rambling thoughts. Normally Miles is more on the silent side of our conversations, less of a conversationalist and more of a looming shadow.

Breathing shakily, he continues, "She had a life outside the horrid one we were condemned to. He started by threatening us, but when that didn't work, he threatened her friends. One day he left her an image of him standing outside of her best friend's window. She snapped. We all knew something was wrong, but she wouldn't tell us because she'd promised to meet him on her own. She thought she could take him alone, beat him there, set up a trap, but he got there first.

"No one blamed themselves more than Vira for not being there. She wasn't blood-related, but she was a part of our family just as much as anyone, and I don't think we've been the same since she died. We were never able to recover her necklace, so that's why it was such a mystery when you moved to town and were suddenly wearing it around your neck."

My fingers jump to my chest where the heart pendant lies. "I had no idea. Ambrose led me to it the first time he showed himself to me."

"That's why Gwen was snooping around. Vira had seen it on you and wanted to be sure it was hers. All of the girls in our family have one. It's like a sort of family crest. Even if they marry out of the family, they're tied to the Draven bloodline for life. My father, Elliot, Lucas, and myself have these."

Miles pulls down the short V-neck of his black shirt, revealing a small tattoo over the left side of his chest. My eyes trace the familiar design, though this one is slightly different from the one on my—Emile's—pendant. His tattoo stems from the token heart, wild branches tracing up his muscle and across the surface of his pec, bleeding onto his shoulder, farther beneath the material than I can see.

"Wow," I breathe.

Miles releases his shirt, jaw clenching once again as he loses himself in thought. Feeling as if I should say something a little more intelligent sounding, I bite my lip, willing my brain to work.

"That's... intense," I relinquish, closing my eyes as the realization sinks in that I've been wearing a necklace that belonged to the late Emile Draven. "You must want it back."

My fingers fumble with the clasp, suddenly wanting it off of me more than ever. That house, this family, the crest... it's all a little bit much, and much, much more than I was bargaining for when he saved my life.

Miles pushes off from his tree, not stopping until he's close enough to really capture my attention. "I believe you found it for a reason. We searched up and down the property for days and you just stumbled upon it in plain sight? That is no accident, but I do think it was fate."

"Fate?" I raise an eyebrow in distaste. "I don't believe in such a thing."

"And yet you ended up being the solution to our problems?"

"We don't know that yet."

"That necklace you found by chance led the hunter to you, then led you to me. He saw the crest and assumed you were one of us." Miles raises his eyebrows, clenching his hands in front of him. "It's too convenient."

"He must have figured out I was human when he got closer," I breathe out, maybe it wasn't so much fate as it was a trap Ambrose set to ensure I'd turn, because somehow he seemed to know how important I would be to his family. It's possible that breaking the curse may finally set him free. He could be at peace.

"He probably figured you'd seen too much and could identify him if left alive. It would have blown their whole operation if you went to the cops." He reaches for my hand, but I pull away without meaning to.

"You mean, the only reason any of this happened to me, was because I'm wearing a necklace that belonged to your dead sister," I accuse, almost every word in that sentence sounding foreign on my tongue. Miles winces at my choice of wording and backs up a step. "That your dead uncle led me to?"

"I'm sorry," he says softly, looking pained. I wish I could be mad at him, but it's not his fault. If I blame anyone it's Ambrose, but even he only seems to be looking out for his family, albeit I'm not the biggest fan of his strategies lately. I don't particularly enjoy having the crap scared out of me every time I close my eyes, but his heart is sort of in the right place. If what Miles says about fate is true, and I am in fact the cure, no matter what happened, we inevitably would have ended up here. There might have been different events or people or actions, but if I'm meant to release the Draven family from their curse, I would have become a vampire one way or another.

At least, that's what I choose to believe, though my peace of mind does nothing to help the matter. It's still real, I'm still in danger of dropping dead if I don't turn or of another clan member discovering my transition state. I'm not sure if Miles and his family have brought their clan up to speed, but from what I gather, they haven't risked getting anyone's hopes up just yet, for fear this is all a hoax.

"I am pissed," I assure him, reaching for his hands. "But I don't blame you. It wouldn't be fair of me to pin this on you."

Miles squeezes my fingers, holding our arms between us like a couple in an old TV show. Sometimes he really shows his age. I grimace and stomp that thought down, preferring not to think too much into the age gap between us. "I did this to you, though. I've given you an unfathomable choice—"

"Which is made every day by people far worse than you or your family. It's made by people who have a choice or have every reason to be happy but decide to kill someone anyway out of jealousy or blind rage. For now, let's just address it as a bridge I'll cross when I get there."

He drags his thumb across my cheek, boring into me with a look that sends chills down my spine. "I've never met anyone quite like you."

My chest aches and the air suddenly becomes thick as morning fog. "You haven't been looking hard enough."

He shakes his head back and forth slowly. "Trust me, I've been looking plenty."

I blink several times, weighing his words. I'm not sure how to respond or what I could possibly say to ease the tension growing between us. I worry that if we get too close, there will be more to lose when we're ripped apart by the inevitable— someone is going to figure out my role in this curse, and then they'll kill me. And I won't take the innocent life of someone in this town. Not in the name of saving myself. People will start asking questions we don't have answers to, or at least, answers that they want to hear.

"I uh, I need to check on Elaine," I say softly, clearing my throat uncomfortably and dashing my eyes up the hill. "She's probably in over her head."

"I'll come," he insists. Panic fills me at his words.

"No," I say, maybe a little too quickly. "I just mean, if she saw what she probably did, I don't know how she'll handle it. So it's, uh, best if you don't. You know, until she's comfortable with everything."

Miles is apprehensive about telling Elaine the truth, and I don't blame him. But in time, she'll make her peace with what they are. And if she meant what she said, that she doesn't want to lose me as a friend, then she'll accept us. And if she's in on the secret… then there's nothing to hide from her anymore. She'll never have to feel the sting of abandonment or envy that often accompanies being on the outside. She'll finally understand why Owen began acting strange and distanced himself, assuming the Dravens found out he was seeing her and warned him away. She'll be part of something bigger…

Or it'll put a target on her back.

~

"It took you long enough." Elaine swings the door open as my fist rises to knock. "I didn't want to run out like that but I-I needed to think."

Closing the door behind me, I take a few unsure steps into her small, beautifully furnished home. She's taking this... well. No one in their right mind should be expected to comprehend what she's just seen. "Understandably."

"Why are you looking at me like I have three heads?" She claws at the hair in her face, resting a hand on her hip in distraught. Okay, maybe she's not taking this as well as I thought. "You just let Miles Draven drink your blood. Are you insane? Swapping blood is intimate. So intimate you've practically already shacked up with him."

"I never—wait, what?"

"You-you can't just let him drink from you, Aspen, you'll be labeled as a blood whore and then any vampire with fangs will want you."

"You didn't leave because you were scared," I assert disbelievingly, jaw slack. "You know."

She purses her lips, suddenly shyer now that she's been outed. "I wasn't sure. I guess I didn't want to admit the stories I'd heard might be true, but last night I knew I couldn't hide from it anymore."

"But they—" I shake my head, piecing together the truth. "They don't know that you know, which is why you left, so they wouldn't figure out that you know 'cause then you'd be in danger from knowing."

"Exactly. Oh God, I'm so glad you understand." Elaine

collapses onto me in a relieved hug, draping her arms across my shoulders carelessly. I'm anything but relieved.

"I can safely say I don't understand. You have some serious explaining to do, Elaine. Starting with how you know the Dravens are vampires." I push her dangling arms off of me and she falls onto the couch with an unsatisfied eye roll.

"I come from a long line of watchers. We help the vampires survive when the humans aren't on their side. We clean up unexplainable messes to keep the humans from asking questions and stumbling across supernatural dangers. I just found out after you moved to town, but even before I knew—" she exhales loudly, "the second you looked at him with those hungry eyes, I knew you were a goner."

I ignore her comments about Miles and his family, focusing on what I need to know. "Does your whole family know?"

"No, just me. I found my ancestor's old journal between the walls in my room. He said things were getting dangerous and he didn't want to bring his children into it, so he withdrew himself from the life to keep them safe. He used to hold so many dangerous things for the Dravens, then the other clans would come for the items, and many of his family members died protecting the vampire's treasure. It's actually really tragic." She props her legs on the coffee table before her, crossing her arms. "At first I thought he was loony, and then I started watching. Paying attention. My family's house is atop the highest hill in our town, which means it overlooks everything. So I watched. And I saw. And I finally understood why my family has lived here for so long. We're the watchers. We're the keepers. Even if we forgot for some time."

"But didn't your ancestor hide the truth for a reason?" I didn't read the journals so I suppose I don't know anything, though I can't help but think the life of superhuman immortals is no life for a meager human, and maybe her ancestor was right to keep his family away. I understand the vampires need allies, just not human ones.

"That was so long ago. Besides, I'm not about to get in bed with the enemy." She shoots me a pointed look, quirking her lips to the side.

Fiddling with my necklace, I sit on the edge of the couch beside her, staring at my muddy feet. "Do you know about—" I pause, nausea clenching my stomach, "Do you know about me?"

Her sharp eyes cast a look of distaste upon me, pure and unhidden judgment. "That you've allowed yourself to be violated by a bloodsucker?"

"Okay that was once to save his life and you know that. But that's not what I'm talking about. Two nights ago I was attacked by a man. A hunter."

"My ancestor wrote a great deal about them. He wasn't a fan." Worry mixes in with her curiosity. She sits up, suddenly more interested in my involvement with the Dravens.

"He kind of killed me." Elaine's eyes grow wide as saucers, her fingers finding my wrists and squeezing. "Miles saved my life, even though he thought he wouldn't be able to—it's a long story—but he turned me."

"You're one of them." She slides away and I find myself doubting her intentions. No way can she want to reclaim her title as watcher and be terrified of their very existence at the same time.

I shake my head, my hair swishing across my shoulders. "Not exactly. I have a choice, and I'm not entirely okay with either outcome."

"Well, I mean now it makes sense why they let you in. I know they don't feed off of humans, so I couldn't figure out what other use you could have. So they're using you? To break the curse."

Seems as though Elaine's ancestor kept mint records of the Draven family. He must have known my own record-keeping ancestor. "He knew it wouldn't work and he still saved me, Elaine. I don't know what to think, but that has to mean something. They're not all bad."

"My ancestor would have protected that family at the cost of his own life, but they couldn't protect him from the other clans. My father's brother died because of their kind and we were in the dark. They staged a car accident, Aspen, to cover it up."

"It wasn't the Dravens, Elaine. They're different."

"It might as well have been. And yes, I know, it's not what I think, they're good people, they protect the humans, blah, blah, blah. I read all about it in the journal and listened to Owen praise them for weeks on end. I didn't believe it then, when I knew nothing, so I certainly don't believe it now. Terrible darkness follows that family. Whatever your ultimatum, choose the option that gets you the hell away from them."

"If it weren't for Miles, I'd be dead. My parents would have lost another child, and my brother another sibling. No matter what happens, I'm grateful for the time I have left."

I hadn't realized I felt that way until the words came pouring out. I'm living on borrowed time because, well, I should be dead. If I hadn't run so fast and so far, if I'd stood frozen staring at the man with the crossbow, Miles may never have sensed my danger. Any slight change in the events of that night might have ended in completely different circumstances.

I would probably be dead right now if that were the case. So whatever the cost, I'm thankful I get the chance to live a little longer than I was meant to.

"You had another sibling?" Elaine asks, looking lost. She stares at me in confusion and pity, knowing whatever the story, it's not a good one.

"No, nothing. Forget I said anything," I whisper, standing up and rushing to the door with Elaine on my heels. I don't know why, I just thought she might understand what I'm going through, being the only other human aware of what's happening in this town. Instead, it feels like I'm being judged and criticized for things that I had no control over.

"You're gonna tell them I know, aren't you?" she accuses, crossing her arms in resentment.

I don't bother telling her Miles is probably outside right now, listening to everything we've said. "You did that when you climbed out the window."

CHAPTER 16

*a*s I predicted, the moment I leave Elaine's house, I find Miles waiting for me a safe distance away. I stop for a brief second on her front steps, then cut off, jogging down the dirt path toward the covered woods.

"Were you listening?" I ask, slowing my pace.

There's no doubt in my mind he followed me. It's as if I can sense his presence. I breathe heavily, resting my hands on my hips. It's astonishing I managed to run so far while being chased and yet find myself winded after jogging no more than a few feet.

"No." He stares ahead at the dancing trees full of lively green leaves that sway in the still summer air. "I trust you."

"If your family asks?" I prod, dipping my chin so he has no choice but to look at me.

His index finger slides beneath the thin strap of my tank top.

"I heard every word." His voice is stolen by the wind as it thrusts past us, eagerly weaving through the tree trunks along the path. "I don't think you're safe at home anymore."

I blink, watching as his finger twists and tugs at the orange material on my shoulder. "Was I ever?"

With Ambrose invading my mind nightly, I've never felt entirely comfortable sleeping in my own bed. He can't kill me because I'm responsible for freeing the Dravens of their curse, yet he stops at no length to harm me any chance he gets. I'm terrified of him, but I have other threats in my life that are much more dangerous than a man who haunts me in my sleep. I have to believe he can't harm me more than he already has or else I'll never know peace.

"Stay with me," Miles says absentmindedly, and I can't help but wonder if, when he looks at me, he remembers the taste of my blood, the feel of his teeth sinking beneath my warm skin.

"No." His hand falters as his eyes shoot to mine, clearly not expecting a rejection. "My family. I won't leave them."

"The hunter's following you, not them," he reminds me, suggesting I'll be putting them in danger if I stay, not if I go.

Standing my ground, I step closer to him so his chest brushes mine with each breath. "Aren't you the one who said a hunter threatened Emile's human friends to get to her? I won't fall prey to his mind games, and I won't run scared. I'm staying."

Peering into his eyes, I notice a small, circular ring around the outer edges of the usually golden color. It's darker with tinges of red lacing through the intricate swirls. He says nothing in response to my defiance, but it's clear he doesn't agree with my choice.

"You want my blood." My voice sounds firm and strong, much more so than I feel as I slide my hand up his chest and to his lips, where my thumb presses firmly against the edge of his teeth. His tongue slides across the pad of my thumb and his eyes darken, hand snatching mine roughly and shoving it away. I rise to my tiptoes and lean in close, pushing away the hair that curls around it. He takes a shaky breath and holds it, unwilling to breathe me in. I press my lips to his ear and say, low and stern, "Control yourself. I know you can."

"I've tasted your blood before… it's not as simple as having self-restraint." He grunts, placing his hands on my shoulders and pushing me away. "You're an addiction, and the hungrier I get, the less control I'll have."

"You've stopped before," I remind him. He could have killed me last night but refrained. He can do it again.

He shakes his head. "That was different. The urge to kill you will only grow stronger."

Frustrated, I close my eyes and turn away from him.

The last possible thing I need to worry about is Miles becoming an Aspen's-Blood addict. Maybe Elaine was right, I never should have let him taste my blood, not while it's in an addictive state. Before, I'd have trusted Miles with my life, but after seeing Ambrose and his passion and aggression toward tasting me, I realize my blood might do more harm than good. After all, there has to be a price when healing someone on the brink of death, just like there is when one becomes a vampire. A life for a life. Health for sanity. I just hope once I change—if I change—that the temptation he feels will disappear along with my life-force.

When I look back to where Miles had been standing, I find he's no longer there. I twist around for a moment before returning my attention to the dirt path and am startled by him standing five feet away from me. I trip over a root sticking up from the ground and curse.

"Could you move like a normal person?" I cry out, standing

up on shaking legs and brushing the dirt from my front. It's coating my clothes and skin, too damp to completely wipe away.

"Maybe I should—" Miles chokes on his words, clenching his fists so hard his knuckles turn ghostly white. He stands a few feet ahead of me, but still close enough to scare me half to death. "I don't want to hurt you."

"If you think you're going to pull that crap where you leave because it's what's best for me, I might just punch you." I swallow, fear creeping up my throat. "I'm staying with my family because it's safest for everyone, but that doesn't mean you can just abandon me."

"I couldn't leave you if I wanted to," he says earnestly, lifting his eyes to meet mine. I gnaw on my inner lip, finding it odd that I'm not afraid of taunting him when he wants to devour me, yet when he tells me he could never leave, terror strikes the core of my being.

Burning flames erupt within my chest as I realize the full depths of the willpower he uses just to hold himself back. "Then what now?"

"Ash." His voice comes out raw. "Any kind weakens us. I won't be able to hurt you."

His chest heaves and his eyes seem to roam me up and down desperately.

"We have an old fireplace," I say stupidly, and to my surprise, my offer isn't laughed at.

"That will work."

"Is there anything that can eradicate the cravings?" I ask, motioning for him to walk ahead of me. I'm fully aware he could zoom around and drain every ounce of blood from my body before I realize he's not in front of me anymore, but I still feel better having an eye on him.

"The blood of a dead animal," he responds tightly and I'm left wondering if this is some sick joke. It must not be, as he continues. "Vampires crave the life-force of other beings, so drinking blood from the deceased will sicken us enough so that we don't hunger for blood even if it's dripping down our faces."

"That's disgusting." I retch, rubbing a hand across my stomach in discomfort. As if the thought of feeding on a human being wasn't sickening enough...

This... this takes the cake.

"Or we could drink their urine."

My eyes widen in disgust. I feel so ill, I'm forced to lean against a nearby tree for support. A moment too late, Miles speaks with humor coating his voice. "I'm only kidding."

I place a hand over my mouth, tasting the remnants of bile in my throat as I gag and clench my stomach. "You're going to hell for that."

He shrugs, unfazed. "I'm going there, regardless."

When we finally arrive at my house, I turn just before we reach the overgrown grass, knowing he doesn't like to be denied. I can't afford for my family to ask questions I can't answer and there's no way I'm allowing him anywhere near my brother when he can't control himself, weak or not.

"Find that dead animal blood." I can hardly speak the words without feeling queasy. "I'll be okay for one night. You won't do much good weakened anyway."

There's no way I can risk him sitting at my bedside while I sleep. Ambrose would be the least of my worries.

Miles closes his eyes, then takes a hesitant step toward me

so everything but him fades away. The sun, the sky, the trees, the grass, the sweet smells of nature I'm always consumed by anymore. He's all there is, filling up every crevice of my world.

"Does your father have any weapons? You should have something to protect yourself with in case the hunter returns." His fingers twist a short piece of blonde hair that hangs in my face, bleached from my recent adventuring with Elaine, or maybe it's from my new lifestyle. Everything about me seems different now. I hardly recognize myself.

"He keeps a gun in the shed," I say, already wondering how I'm going to explain that or sneak it into the house unnoticed. Our back door sticks so I'll need to walk around the house, which I can't say I'm too comfortable with, considering recent events.

"Get it. Just in case," he instructs, and I nod, forging several excuses in my head as to why I need my father to get it for me. I'm sure I can come up with something without arousing suspicion, but I'm probably better off just getting it myself.

Miles watches me expectantly, and when I nod, he steps away regretfully. "I won't leave until I at least know you're inside."

My chest pounds dangerously as I nod again, mirroring his intense stare.

"That goes both ways." No way am I going to sit alone with my father's shotgun wondering if Miles made it home this time or if he was captured once again by a hunter, lying helpless in a ditch somewhere. "By the time I reach the kitchen, the phone better be ringing with your call."

I back inside the house, closing our screen door without taking my eyes off of him. Once the door is closed and I've slid the lock into place, he smiles, disappearing as if he were never here at all.

Then the phone rings.

CHAPTER 17

*J*t's early evening when Dallas finds me stretched out on my bed, writing away in a small, carved journal, lost to the world by my thoughts. I'm unaware of how long he stands there watching me, but the second I notice him, I slam the cover closed and slip it beneath my bedsheets.

My brows raise expectantly as I wait to be chastened or treated like a child by my same-age brother. We may look completely different, but only six minutes separate us from one another.

"I knew you made one friend, but holy crap, Aspen." He whistles, scratching the back of his head. "I've got to admit, I was a tad surprised waking up to an entire small family in our living room."

"You knew who they were?" I ask worriedly, mind scrambling for possible excuses and defenses. Giving their real names probably wasn't the smartest move, especially if Dallas has heard more about their family than I have.

"Not explicitly, but I've been to town before. I see how they're looked at, how they watch everyone. It's like they travel in a pack." He shakes his head, searching my expression for something that might give him solace, relief that there's a perfectly good explanation as to why they spent the night. "The townsfolk are scared of them."

"They're not bad people," I assure him, crossing my legs stubbornly and fixing him with what he likes to call a mom-stare.

"I never said they were." He raises his eyebrows at my quick jump to their defense. "But I don't think they're the kind of people you should be spending your time with."

Mild annoyance surfaces at his eagerness to keep me from danger. Where was he the night I was attacked or the past few days when I've been struggling with changes that almost make me miss puberty. Has he forgotten about all the nights I lost sleep worrying over him, worrying he would become like our brother?

Dallas's night terrors only woke me up at first, and then they progressed to the point where I couldn't sleep at all because I was holding him in my arms to keep the fear at bay long enough for him to doze off. I was too afraid to close my eyes because every time I did, he'd start screaming again. Or what about his lot of friends back home that used to trash the town at night, forcing parents to make sure their children were in before dark because the scary boys would come by and terrify them. "I don't think who I spend my time with is any of your business."

"As if what happens to you won't affect this entire family." His voice raises a few octaves and he holds his breath, placing his palms together in a begging motion. "You don't want to be responsible for throwing Mom off the deep end."

"Derek, it was an innocent sleepover in our living room." I

clamp my mouth shut with instant shame, and heat creeps across my cheeks. "I'm so sorry, it just came out."

"This is exactly what I mean. You're being reckless, and at first I'm sure it was fun, but now you're losing control."

"I'm living my life." I swallow back the tears pushing their way to the surface. He has no room to lecture me on losing control. It wasn't until after Derek attacked us that Dallas finally straightened himself out. He was traumatized by what our brother did, and it opened his eyes to who he was in danger of becoming. "I love you, but I can't hold myself back to protect you forever."

Dallas looks at me as though I'm a stranger invading his home in the dead of the night. Just as well, I don't recognize the look I see in his eyes, and it scares me because just moments ago, I referred to him as Derek. I spoke to him like I had our older brother when he was slipping through the cracks and no one but me would acknowledge something was seriously wrong with him. The more time that had passed, the longer I spent lying wide awake at night thinking about all the things I could have done to save him, all the things my parents could have done to show him he would be special whether he could play soccer or not, because that's all he'd wanted; to know he'd still be someone without the number thirty-six jersey on his back. At a certain point, I started to wonder if it wasn't the pills that drove him mad. Is it possible the very thing we blamed for the destruction of my brother merely brought out a side of him kept dormant all those years?

"At least I finally know how you really feel," Dallas scoffs, storming out of my room. I fling my body from the bed and chase after him. When I reach him, he's at the front door, shoving his foot in a tennis shoe.

"That's not what I meant," is all I can manage. My upper lip trembles, breaking out in a sweat.

The pills pushed Derek over the edge. I don't want to be the thing that pushes Dallas over, too.

"Don't bother." He jerks around so fast I stumble backward into a chair. He laughs spitefully at my clumsiness and distraught reaction. "Good luck with whatever you need the gun under your bed for."

Before I've even processed what he's said, my six minutes and forty-one seconds older brother storms out of the house.

All I can hope is the psycho stalking me doesn't set his sights on Dallas instead. Though, maybe it's for the best if Dallas leaves

There's a good chance he's better off the farther he is away from me.

CHAPTER 18

*a*round quarter to eleven, the house phone rings and I spring from my bed with speed I didn't realize I possessed. I'm the only one in my family that's given out this number, so if the ringing wakes up my parents, I'll be the one who gets blamed.

I've been doing everything in my power not to fall asleep. Every time my eyes drifted closed, I forced them open again, unwilling to rest my head until Dallas walks through the door, cooled off from his long walk in the wilderness. Except he hasn't come back yet.

I'm scared of something happening to him, but I'm not dumb enough to chase after him in the dead of night. It's me they want, so I have to believe he found a place to stay with friends I know he doesn't have.

"Hello?" I whisper, sliding down the chipped yellow wall in our kitchen, feeling the tension of the spiral phone cord protest.

"I think we need to talk." My chest releases at the sound of Elaine's apologetic voice, and I clutch it in relief. For a moment, I was worried I'd fallen asleep and this was another sick game orchestrated by Ambrose. I envisioned his long slender fingers reaching out through the phone and clawing my neck. "Aspen?"

Her voice jerks me from my terror, leaving me breathless and shaking.

"I'm here," I say weakly, tucking my chin to my knees. "Sorry, my brother and I got in a horrible fight."

"Wanna talk about it?" she offers hopefully. There's a rustling on her end, and I assume she's shifting the phone between her cheek and shoulder, probably cozy in her bed without a care in the world. Meanwhile, I'm one skipping heartbeat away from having a premature heart attack.

Quirking my lips to the side, I close my eyes and breathe evenly to calm my nerves. Then I sit up, deciding that letting my guard down isn't the safest bet. Anyone or anything could sneak up on me. "Not particularly."

Elaine laughs compassionately. "Well, you sound stressed."

I'm not stressed, I want to say, *I'm terrified.*

I have this constant paranoia coursing through me, like at every moment someone can see me, might be watching me through the small window above the sink, from between the bars of missing blinds on our back door, or the cracks in the floorboards.

"Anyway," she continues when my silence proves to be response enough to satisfy her. "I just wanted to apologize for earlier. Personal opinions aside, what you did for Miles was really brave. So long as he deserves your sacrifices, I can stomach them."

I roll my eyes as I huff out a laugh. "Thanks?"

"You're welcome," she sasses, as if she's done me some huge

favor at her own expense. "Are you okay, though? For real? That was some pretty deep shit last night, and I didn't think about it until later."

"Whether I'm awake or asleep I'm being tormented." I bite my tongue. The last thing I want to do is weigh Elaine down with worries of my safety the way Dallas used to lay all of his problems on me.

"Asleep?"

"Never mind, forget I said anything."

"Uh uh. You can only pull that card once a day. Now, what do you mean asleep?"

My jaw clenches as I scold myself for opening my mouth. I've already told her this much, I might as well fill her in on the rest of my dreary life. Besides, it actually might do me some good to confide in someone else about it. Perhaps she can make sense of what I'm going through. At the end of the day, Ambrose was a Draven, and from what I've gathered, a wrongfully cursed and killed one. It's going to be hard to convince anyone in that family he's causing me harm, even if the proof is evident. "Ambrose Draven—"

"Shut up," she interrupts before I can say another word. "The one who went crazy in your house and killed himself?"

I squeeze my eyes shut, willing reality to fade for a few moments, but it never goes away. "He's haunting my dreams. And when I wake up, what he does to me is still there. That's how I knew to heal Miles with my blood. He attacked me and said something like, 'the blood of a transitioner always makes a vampire feel brand new.'"

"You think he was trying to help save Miles," Elaine says wearily. I don't blame her, this is a lot. And if Ambrose is willing to harm me to save his family, how much danger am I really in?

"Either that, or he's psychotic without a purpose and I just got lucky." I peer around the room at the flickering lights and creaking ceiling beams, feeling the eerie suspicion that Ambrose watches me even while I'm awake.

"When did you start having these dreams of him?"

I pause, thinking this over for a second before it occurs to me. "They actually started the night before I met you."

A mere few hours before I heard the Draven name for the first time.

The front door flies open and I jump to my feet unsteadily. I crumple to the floor with a sigh upon seeing Dallas's face. He stares at me with a hard expression, then after a few moments shakes his head and disappears into our rooms. It only makes sense that we shared a womb and now we're forced to suffer each other's company by essentially sharing a sleeping space.

"What was that?" Elaine asks, bringing me back to the present.

"Dallas. He's home," I inhale slowly. I'm still furious with him, but knowing he's alive and well gives me a rightful reason to hold on to my anger. "I'll call you tomorrow. I'm going to try and talk him down."

"Good luck." And with those well wishes, I'm left listening to a dial tone.

"We need to talk," I holler as I follow his path with my arms crossed in defiance.

I've got insane dead people haunting me in my sleep and vampire hunters trying to kill me when I'm awake—I need the small bit of serenity that is my brother and his obnoxious conversations about stupid things I don't have to think about.

"You're right," he agrees, to my surprise. He unties his shoes and slips them off, walking past me to return them to the small, wooden shelf by our front door.

"Really?" I ask hopefully, watching as he walks by. He sounds calmer, but the look in his eyes is still rabid.

He comes back around the corner with his chest puffed and his shoulders pulled back, a look of pure rage splayed across the face I used to think resembled an innocent child's when he cried at night.

"You know what?" He pauses in front of me before going back into his room. "I have nothing to say to you."

"But you—" My words fall short, as does his agreement that we need to talk. I spin around so fast that I lose my balance and have to grab onto the doorframe.

"Do we have any bottled water?" He asks casually, cocking his head to the side. He watches me intently, waiting for a response as if we're not in the middle of an argument.

The disbelief in my voice is hard to miss. "Not in the fridge. I think there's some in the pantry though. Dallas—"

My brother walks toward me with his mouth open to speak but stops short, expression turning to a scowl as the wheels in his head most clearly come to a halt and begin turning in the opposite direction. "Can you move?"

Biting my lip in frustration, I flail my arms wildly, complexed and utterly confused as to why my brother is giving me such whiplash. This takes multiple personalities to an altogether different level. "Walk around me."

Moments later the fridge slams closed, followed by Dallas storming back through the threshold separating our rooms. His furious and carelessly loud stomping shifts into a casual stride toward his bed where he drops down and crosses his ankles. Bewildered, I move closer to him so I can get a better look at his face.

He's comfortably sprawled on his bed, scrolling through his phone and feeling the nightstand for his corded earbuds that he uses to block out noise when he wants to focus. Shifting my weight, I stare at him until he looks up, just about to stick the second bud in his ear. "What's up?"

Something tickles my nose, and I rub it with my fingers as a burn tingles up the bridge. I sneeze, once, then twice, and rub my watering eyes. Scrunching it up and down, I say, "Something's burning my nose."

"Bless you," he says almost simultaneously, laughing. "Welcome to my crib, where the air is stuffy and the soot is thick."

"The ash," I whisper, raising my fingers to my lips and averting my eyes to the large fireplace. A few half-burned logs lie cold and dead at the base, and it's dusted in gray-looking sand. "It's the ash."

My brother is silent for a moment, probably trying to decide whether I'm messing with him or genuinely astonished by the allergy-inducing particles in the air. "What?"

He's not just in my dreams. He's in this house. He's affecting all of us.

"Can I sleep in here tonight?"

My eyes trace the soft swirls on the ceiling, chipped from years of water damage and lack of being tended to. The poor condition goes to show the absence of care and effort put into this place since my ancestors left it to the wolves.

I rest my eyes, listening to the sounds of night—crickets, wind, never-ending rain. The house creaks and moans stubbornly against the storm outside, lightning being the only source of light illuminating Dallas's tiny room.

I roll to the side anxiously, staring into my room from the stiff mattress on the floor that squeaks just as much as the house itself.

Sitting up straight, I peer through the darkness as a shape comes into focus. There's a silhouette standing in the doorway. I scoot back until I'm pressed against Dallas's bed frame, but he doesn't stir. The power went out a few hours ago, and as a result, so did his lamp.

Lightning strikes and the room erupts in a bright glow, forcing me to shield my eyes. When I open them again, the shape is gone and darkness retakes its place.

Sleep hasn't come any easier to me knowing that Ambrose —*probably*—can't reach me surrounded by all of this ash, but instead, it makes falling asleep even more frightening. If he can't torment me, then what? Will he go after my parents? Are they safe? Are any of us really safe?

I hear the floor above me creak as soft footsteps move about, causing my heartbeat to rise at an alarming rate. I'm almost positive neither of my parents are awake at this hour, let alone walking around. It's just the wind.

The stairs creak next, and I can't help it, I rise from the mattress, slowly sneaking through our rooms to peer out into the living room. I don't see anyone, but that doesn't necessarily mean I'm alone. My fingers close around the door handle and I'm careful to avoid any spots on the floor that groan loud enough to alert the intruder to my presence. When there are no sounds or movements, I step into the living room clutching the sandy powder in my hand, careful not to let too much fall between the cracks of my fingers to the floor.

"Who's there?" I whisper nervously, reaching for my father's shotgun, which I stashed behind the door before bed. I really hope it's not one of my parents in the kitchen or else this will be very hard to explain.

Gnawing on my lip, I round the corner into the kitchen and catch sight of my reflection in the old mirror hanging on the wall. My eyes glow in the darkness, the mirror reflecting a light I cannot see. I move closer and my pounding heart protests every step until I'm directly in front of it. I've learned my lesson about touching anything that draws me to it, but the last time I got this close, I saw Ambrose's face staring back at me.

The room lights up, revealing a tall, pale figure over my shoulder, smiling with bloody teeth and a slow ooze dripping down his chin. He reaches for me, and I let out a whimper, feeling the pressure of a hand on my shoulder. I turn quickly, but he's gone. I silently pray the ash is keeping him from getting too close to me. Except I'm awake, aren't I? I didn't fall asleep. I couldn't have...

But the lamp is out...

The lightbulbs above me spark and shatter, sending pieces of glass flying all across the room, slicing through my skin. I drop to the ground, draping my arms over my head and trying to keep a firm hold on the ash and gun, too paralyzed with fear to use either. I stash the ash in my pocket so both hands are free to use the gun.

"Leave me alone," I cry, shifting to my knees and holding it across my body. Ambrose is nowhere in sight, but I can feel him. He's still here. He's never far from me.

The front door flies open and I jump to my feet, swinging

the long barrel toward the intruder. He's fast though, moving toward me and snatching the gun from my hands before I get the chance to aim. I don't let go easily though, and his jerking motion causes my foot to slide on the rug, knocking me to the ground.

Before I fall, I manage to get some of the ash from my pocket and throw it in his face. I can't see him very well in the darkness, but it looks like his hands clutch his face as he groans in agony. I scramble away, but he grabs my ankle before I can get to the door—not that I'd necessarily be any safer outside.

"Don't kill me," I yell, grabbing onto the base of the couch, though I'm not sure what good that will do.

"Relax, Van Helsing," a strained voice replies, releasing my ankle and flipping me over so I can see his face.

Coughing violently, I widen my eyes and wipe the ash off my sweaty palms. "Elliot?"

He mutters something unintelligible and stumbles toward the sink, which he turns on and sticks his head under to remove the particles lodged in his eyes. "This is why we don't involve humans."

"I'm not exactly human anymore, thanks to my connection to your family," I retort, stretching out my sore legs and back while trying to catch my breath. In the meantime, I scan the room for remaining signs of Ambrose. "What are you doing here? I didn't think any of you wanted to help me."

"We don't." Elliot throws the now-dirty dishrag in the trash instead of the sink and walks toward me angrily. If I thought he didn't like me before...

I scoff, disgusted with his bluntness. My life is on the line because of his stupid family curse, the least he could do is pretend I'm not the bane of his existence. "Then why were you outside my house?"

Elliot sucks on his teeth, anger radiating from his pores.

"Miles cares for you," he says, and it's clear to me why he's the leader. The way he carries himself bleeds power. "He would hate himself if anything happened to you, and I must protect my brother."

"Well just... don't come in guns blazing next time," I scold, running a hand through my tangled hair, hoping he doesn't point out that I'm the only one with a gun. Then I say, so I don't seem ungrateful, "It was Ambrose, I think. He can't touch me when I'm awake but can still make contact."

This was probably payback for figuring out his weakness. I was an idiot to leave Dallas's room just because I thought I heard someone in the house. If someone had truly broken in, they would have come for me. I wouldn't have had to seek them out.

"I don't remember asking. I'll be keeping watch outside," Elliot replies, slamming the front door before I realize he's gone.

"Right," I say to myself, heading to rinse my hands in the sink before hurrying back to the safety of Dallas's room in case Ambrose decides he's ready for round two.

CHAPTER 19

I spent most of last night lying awake in the dark, curled up under a large throw blanket shielding me from the outside world. The one prominent thought in my head being that Ambrose is in my house. Not just my dreams or my nightmares. He's walking the halls, watching, listening, observing.

Controlling.

I'm not sure what I thought the explanation would be when I found out how he was entering my subconscious, but I never thought it would include him being more present in our lives than I ever could have predicted. And despite going about my life in these six, barely furnished rooms with a feeling of vacancy on a daily basis, processing the idea that Ambrose is somehow architecting our emotions makes me feel as if tiny bugs are crawling underneath my skin. The home I once thought of as vacant and cold suddenly feels as if there's more life walking through these walls than I ever thought possible.

"Can I borrow your phone?" I bite my bottom lip, smiling sweetly at my brother.

Dallas doesn't look especially pleased about handing over his prized possession. When we lived in Colorado, he had so many game consoles I couldn't keep track of them all. But after Derek, we couldn't afford to bring them all with us, given we had very little time to run and nothing but the deed to this house and the clothes on our backs. Once we began receiving threats, I'd packed a bag—I've always been a little paranoid that way—in case the occasion arrived where we had to disappear. Even still, it was impossible for me to save everything. His phone is the only thing he has left of his old, technologically run world. Mine was broken during our travels.

"Please tell me you got the dead animal blood?" are the first words to spill from my lips when I hear Miles's voice on the other end of the line.

I'm beginning to realize I can't do this alone, not that I ever fantasized about a world where I could. Truth is, even though Miles and his family are the reason I'm in this mess to begin with, I don't think I'd want it any other way. If it weren't for him, my mind would have drowned in overwhelming circumstances long before I was killed.

When we came here, I was at my breaking point. Sure, I was relieved to get away from the small town that suffocated us for years even though it was all I'd ever known, but getting away doesn't necessarily mean I was escaping. Not only did I lose my older brother to psychosis, but I lost my entire world to his consequences. He got off easy. Jail. A shorter sentence than he deserves, too, thanks to me. It was my family and I that really had to—have to—live with the repercussions of what he's done. I was depressed. Lost. Miles gave me the opportunity to be so much more than my past.

"Not yet. It isn't safe to hunt at night, so Vira convinced me to wait," Miles says with a smile in his voice. That was no doubt Vira and Vanesa's poor attempt at keeping Miles away from me. "You sound worried, what's wrong?"

I peek through the curtain of hair shielding my face and examine my brother, who's knee-deep in his closet searching for his extra pencil sharpener. He seems completely occupied, but I would bet money he's trying his hardest to overhear my conversation. Talking like this in front of him is in no way assisting my case regarding the Dravens and their saint-like behavior, so I make sure to speak softly. It's actually quite ironic considering they're more closely related to the devil.

"I think Ambrose is controlling Dallas. I think he's controlling all of us," I tell Miles, lowering my voice as I make my way to the window parallel to mine. After a quick scan of the yard, I conclude that Elliot is gone. He must have left this morning so no one would figure out what he was really doing last night. God-forbid anyone finds out he helped me.

"What do you mean?" A thick layer of concern coats his tone as movement on his end becomes evident.

Tucking my hair behind my ear, I glance over my shoulder to make sure Dallas still isn't listening. "I didn't recognize him last night with the way he was acting, and then he went into his room and was absolutely fine, as if one of the worst fights we've ever had didn't happen. There's a fireplace in his room."

"You think the ash is keeping Ambrose from controlling him in there."

"Am I crazy?"

Miles releases a breathy laugh, making my hairs stand on edge. "Absolutely."

Moments later, there's a knock on the door and I rush to it, tossing my brother's phone on his bed without hanging up.

"But you also happen to be right," Miles says, standing in front of me now.

My eyes widen considerably, and I check behind me to ensure my parents aren't awake yet. "Are you sure being here is such a good idea?"

His silence is my response, though I'm not sure if I should take it as a good one or bad as he pushes past me into the house.

For the rest of the day, we search through my grandfather's files, full of images of Miles's family. In some of them, he's just a boy, though as the dates near 1803 he begins to look eerily similar to the version of him I know now, making me believe he was turned a year or two before the curse took effect. I shudder, thinking about how different things would be had he waited a little longer.

I'm not sure what exactly we're looking for, but Miles seems to think he'll know when we find it.

"I mean, he lived and died here, isn't that enough for his spirit to have... lingered?" I ask, throwing down a pile of papers and massaging my temples. Miles is looking a little worse for wear as well, though his headache isn't so much from researching the past as it is from being in the presence of ash. I insisted it wasn't necessary, but he made me sneak a bowl of it from the fireplace downstairs and put it between us as insurance. I don't know why he has such a strenuous time trusting himself.

"In theory... yes. But something keeps bothering me about how you ended up here," Miles exhales, glancing at the ash like it's the devil's spawn. "His connection is stronger than it should be."

"My ancestor owned the house. It's not entirely baffling," I say, yanking back my hair in attempt to ease my escalating headache. The ponytail loops through my matted hair, pulling tight on my scalp before I return to scanning the documents.

Miles reaches across the stacks of blue folders and finds my hand beneath the thick of them. "Do you want to take a break?"

I bite my lip in consideration, roaming his pale skin and sunken eyes.

"I'm not the one sweating through my clothes." I flip my hand so I can give his a light squeeze. "Why are you putting yourself through this torture?"

"You need my help," he says meaningfully, as if that's all there is. As if helping me and keeping me safe is worth his own demise. It's astounding to me how willing he is to put my needs beyond his own. I must admit, it's also quite frightening. "Aspen, there is nothing I wouldn't do for you."

Nodding shortly, I focus on the endless stacks of illegible handwriting and blurred photographs that are so frail I'm surprised they haven't desiccated. Even if the answers do lie within these pages, there's a fairly good chance I won't be able to read them when they're found.

Desperate to eradicate the deafening silence and change the subject to one that's not so heavy, I say, "I didn't think cameras were invented until 1816 or so."

Miles smirks mischievously, eyeing the small square in his hand. "That's what we wanted you to think."

I squint at him, utterly perplexed as to why they'd want to keep such an invention to themselves, until the realization dawns on me.

"You wanted to immortalize yourselves because you're… wow. Frozen in time. Clever," I scoff, thumbing the edge of the paper I'm only pretending to read at this point. There's nothing like a still image to capture the eternality of a vampire.

"It's getting late," Miles says, standing slowly. The sound of his chair squeaking on the hardwood floor pierces the air like a gunshot. "I'll let you know I've made it home."

I watch as he walks limply around the doorframe, grabbing onto it for support. I don't like the idea of him leaving in such a weak state. Actually, I'm not entirely fond of him leaving at all.

Last night was the first in weeks that Ambrose didn't invade my head, minus the wretched night I spent unconscious with Miles and Vanesa. Which makes sense in a way—I was too far from the house for Ambrose to reach me. He's tethered to something here, I've just got to figure out what. And judging from the events of last night, the ash does protect me so long as I stay in Dallas's room, and when I'm awake, it's harder for Ambrose to reach me.

With each step Miles takes away from me, another lump of fear molds in my stomach, piling one after another until the pressure is too much. I tap anxiously on the table, fiddling with my pen and biting my lip.

"Come by anytime, hon!" Mom hollers and I visualize her fake grin, glass of lemonade in hand.

Reality sets in as the sound of the door creeping closed kicks my butt in gear and sends me flying down the stairs. My father takes up the entirety of the couch, passed out with an empty bottle of beer resting between his pecs. From the looks of the tinted stains on his deep green shirt, the bottle wasn't empty when he first placed it there.

My mom is exactly how I imagined she'd be.

Thrusting the door open, I let it slam behind me as I jog down our rickety front porch steps at a daring speed.

"Miles?" I call, knowing he couldn't have gotten that far. His vampiric hearing would have picked up my speeding heartbeat and footsteps on the stairs. I step into the tall grass, looking around furiously, praying he's still here.

"Go back inside."

I turn, not the least bit surprised he managed to sneak up behind me. The more time I spend around his abilities, the more used to them I grow.

"You're stronger than you think you are." I step forward, though it doesn't do much to close the gaping hole he's keeping between us.

"Even on my hungriest days, I've never craved a human's blood so much." He watches my feet as they step closer to him, one by one until we're an arm's length apart. He shudders, trying to withdraw, but I grab his wrist, and although he's strong enough to pull away, the gravity of his desire keeps him rooted in place. His eyes flash warnings I wholeheartedly choose to ignore, though I do release his arm so as not to overwhelm him.

He zeroes in on my chest, listening to my pounding heart and watching me with distinct attention to detail, almost as a predator would its prey.

"We never figured out how to stop Ambrose. I'm worried for my family," I say, which is true but not the reason I chased after him.

Miles eyes me with suspicion, breathing heavily like he's out of breath, even though the ash's effect has mostly worn off. He says nothing as he watches me, watches my averting eyes and fiddling fingers, shifting weight and restless lips. He knows fear isn't fueling me at the moment, and I think that's exactly what scares me into keeping my mouth shut.

Mustering the strength I knew he had, Miles moves toward me, gently placing his hands against my cheeks, so warm it's as if his touch burns through me. His fingers reach to the back of my neck and push deeply into the knots formed from countless hours of sleeping on a lumpy mattress. Then he leans in slowly, pressing a kiss to the top of my forehead just below my hairline. His lips linger for a moment before he pulls away, just enough so he can speak without his words being muffled against my skin.

"You don't want me to leave," he murmurs into my hair, breathing me in. Shakily, his hands circle my back and pull me to him. My forearms press against his stomach as the space between us narrows. The cool circulation around us makes me shiver, which in return causes Miles to tremble hungrily. "Why can't you just say it?"

I search his soulful eyes, wondering how a man with a heart so kind could feel this kind of pain when near someone he cares about. My mouth slacks as if words are about to be spoken, and yet I can't bring myself to say them.

There's a part of me that is afraid of what may happen if I ask Miles Draven to stay. It will no longer be him wanting to protect me, watch over me, and help with research. If I ask him to stay, it will be because I want him to, and in return, he'll stay because he wants to.

There's no uncrossing that line. Up until now, we relied on the legitimate reasons we needed to stay together. A mutual benefit of sorts.

What are we when all of our excuses are gone?

Miles's hands ease up my waist and around my shoulders to

my neck, where they pause on the shallow scar where he bit me, until he drags his fingers across my jawline to my chin where they linger. My eyes are focused on the centimeters of dirt between his shoes and my bare feet. He then dips his neck so our mouths are dangerously close together. I fight against the heavy weight on my eyelids to find his gaze, discovering the push and pull ensuing within him. There is an internal war progressing within Miles Draven, and both its victor and casualty could very well be me.

"I'll come back," he promises thickly, moving so close our noses brush, sending sparks of anticipation across my abdomen. Just when I think he's finally giving in, cold wind wraps its arms around me, squeezing me in the glimmering light of the setting sun. Miles disappears before my eyes, leaving me standing barefoot and alone in the tall grasses swaying to the songs of the wind.

CHAPTER 20

I feel like an intruder in my own home.

Where every wall ends, curving into a new room, I pause, listening, waiting, preparing for the worst. And in those waiting moments my heart goes limp, terrified, paranoid.

Knowing the truth about Ambrose has me rethinking sound possibilities and replacing them with vast uncertainties. My father sobered up just long enough to dig out the records I so desperately needed to help me uncover the truth hidden behind the highly raised walls of this town. My father also hasn't been without a beer in his hand since Derek attempted to commit murder, so how in the world did he manage to momentarily forget about his addiction?

Exactly how much of our lives does the ghost of Ambrose Draven control?

In a desperate attempt to reclaim my mind, I begin separating the paperwork and images we've already sorted through from those we haven't begun to dissect. There are more newspaper clippings than anything, actually. I had assumed my ancestor only kept the one of Ambrose because he knew him—he did, after all, abandon this place forever and move to the states right after Ambrose went mad. I thought maybe the two of them were friends, so I imagine it would have been quite hard for him to watch his friend's mind disintegrate before his eyes, with nothing to do but let it happen. Though from looking at this alarmingly large collection, it seems he kept small squares of every death in town, or at least what seems to be every death possible. There can't be more than what he's saved given the extensive number of them so close together. It's not possible for there to have been more deaths than those spread before me or else there wouldn't be a town left standing.

There were three deaths within the span of a few weeks, all seeming to be unrelated. Months later, the killings picked up again, these ones more similar, more calculated.

On November 12, 1802, a young couple drowned in a lake after a seemingly awful fight. Authorities believed the wife had murdered the husband after he hit her and then drown herself in shame.

November 24, 1802, two young children were found face-down in the same lake, bruises around their necks as if they'd been strangled.

December 6th the same year, a woman was murdered and drug out to the lake where her body was abandoned, left to be devoured by wildlife just like the others.

And another on the 18th and the 30th.

People in this town had been dropping like flies and none of them seem to be supernatural deaths, meaning the killer could very well have been human. My stomach churns uneasily, not liking the direction of my thoughts. These articles are almost like a murderer's souvenirs. Why else save them?

Authorities Scramble to Catch the Twelve-Day Killer
The words 'Twelve-Day Killer' are no stranger to
Ichorye town locals as the hunt for a cold-blooded killer
continues into the dead of night on December 30th.

Authorities have been chasing their tails over the recent
murder spree, which they assume is being committed by
one of our own. A statement from local police revealed
evidence that the murders aren't random, and seem
personal and strategically planned.

"We have a very well-educated coroner, and he believes
these murders are specific and precise, slightly
different between each victim. We've figured out the
pattern and by morning, the son of a bitch will be
locked away for life, which is more than he deserves in
my opinion." Chief Troy goes on to insist that by
midnight tonight, the killer will have been
apprehended.

Clearly, no love is lost there as the time he's chosen
reflects that of the killer's M.O., killing every twelve
days. Meanwhile, the Ichorye community is in a frenzy
preparing for the next attack.

"My paper boys didn't show up today. Parents wouldn't
let 'em,'" says local newspaper editor Randall Kent.

He's not the only one struggling to generate business
because people are too afraid to leave their homes. Still,
the killer manages to lure his victims to the lake, given

there's no evidence they were captured or forced there against their will.

We can only hope an end is put to this tonight.
Otherwise, the small population of Ichorye is going to become quite a bit smaller.

Attached to the back of the article is a square image of what looks to be the Draven family.

I recognize Vanesa right away. Even young, she had lanky legs and eyes that bore straight into your soul. Vira looks cynical as always, though I suppose I wouldn't expect anything less from her. Danielle looks too young to even be in this picture. She must have remained human long after the photograph was taken. Lucas and Elliot, on the other hand, are frozen in time, unchanging in the past two hundred years. A man and woman I don't recognize stand on the far left of the frame and judging by their looks, they must be the siblings' parents. It isn't Edgar that catches my eye, though.

On the opposite end of the photo is a girl with long, wavy hair that I don't recognize. She's looking deeply into the eyes of a boy, and her hand scrunches his face affectionately as her infectious grin spreads to my own. Even within the black and white photograph, the closeness they hold for one another is undeniable. It's as if their eyes shine for the other's. I flip over the photograph, reading the scribbled note:

Covert Lodge—Edgar, Natalia, Vira, Vanesa, Elliot, Danielle, Lucas, Miles, Emile, and Ambrose Draven.

The young boy with the lively eyes and impenetrable smile is Ambrose.

My throat constricts at the image of him so innocent and happy—the man I've seen is none of those things. In many ways, my heart aches for him and what he's become. When it comes down to it, he was a good man trying to save humanity from the clutches of his monster. Ambrose didn't choose the life he was given. In fact, I'm not convinced any of the Dravens wanted immortality.

I've never stopped to wonder how they came to be what they are. It clearly wasn't a tragedy and it wasn't all at once if Danielle remained human up until the year Ambrose died, presumably right before the curse took effect.

I find myself lingering on Emile's dark eyes and devilish grin. She looks wicked in the way Vira does, a perfect statue with the eyes of Medusa. I imagine they were a lot alike.

Ambrose clutches her hip with one hand, the other tugging at the all-too-familiar necklace she wears. My necklace. I find it sickening that he led me to the very object his once-lover wore.

"Aspen, I'm running to town, do you want to come?" Dallas calls from the bottom of the stairs. He's been in a much better mood today, which leaves me to believe Ambrose either knows I've figured it out or is taking a mental break to regain his strengths. I can't fathom the toll it must take on his sanity—or lack thereof—to control a household of emotions and penetrate someone's dreams on a daily basis.

"Give me two minutes."

My heart soars at the possibility of getting away from this wretched place until Miles returns. He never said how long he would be gone, and I'm starting to worry he's not coming back. Regardless, the less time I have to spend here, the better.

Tossing the image into one of the many boxes, I rush down the stairs, taking them two at a time. Dallas offers me a sandwich in the kitchen before we go, and my growling stomach won't let me refuse. As I reach for it, I freeze, staring absently as recognition clicks together the pieces I've been looking for in all of the wrong places.

"Holy shit," I breathe, ignoring the sandwich Dallas is trying to shove into my hands. "Hold on."

I trip on my feet as I stagger back up the stairs and into the study, knocking several boxes off of the table in the process. So much for my organization attempts.

I growl in anger, sifting through the piles of paper I spent so much wasted time putting away, until I come across the photograph. I noticed a man in the mirror before, holding up a camera, and I thought it was possible he was the previous owner, maybe someone in my family. What I was too distracted to pay attention to was the possibility of me seeing his reflection at all in the small, circular mirror hanging on the kitchen wall, directly next to the back door with a thin crack snaking up the dead center. Looking almost as if it hasn't been touched in over two hundred years.

Goose bumps rain down on my pale skin, making me shiver in the suddenly crisp air. That mirror has been in my house for as long as I can remember. Mom told me once that she found it in a box in the attic and thought it way too pretty to be hidden away from the world.

That's how we wound up here. How my father suddenly stumbled across the deed to this house. He's a lot of things, but a businessman has never been one of them. Knowing him, he would have thought the official deed was a car receipt.

Everything that happened—it was all an elaborate ploy to bring us here so I could break the curse. Ambrose made sure I found the necklace, knowing it placed a target on my back, he kept my mom sedated and my father medicated, he even played on Dallas's love for art, making certain none of them would get in my way.

The picture falls from my hand, floating melodically to the floor, soft as a feather. My jaw clenches tight as I think of all the things in my life that would have been different had he not stolen our free will. How many of our decisions were truly ours? How long has he been manipulating my family?

I stomp into the kitchen with a head clearer than ever, grab the tacky mirror off the wall, and slam it to the ground with all of my strength. Shards of glass slice through the air, skidding across the floor and through the small cracks in the wood. It's safe to assume we won't be walking barefoot anymore.

Mom screams, falling back into the counter with a look of terror in her eyes. In my blind rage, I must've missed her standing there, pouring another glass of lemonade.

"Aspen, what the hell?" Dallas stands behind me with his palms pressed to his temples, eyes wide as saucers. "What did you do?"

He looks to Mom, rushing to her side and pulling her to his chest. "Shhh, Mom, it's okay," he soothes, massaging the back of her neck all the while pinning me with a death glare.

"It fell." I shrug, looking down at my legs. A few tiny pieces of glass wedged their way into the skin around my ankles and small trickles of blood run down them, seeping into the top of my short socks.

Father is sitting up on the couch with a look of pure malice lining his expression. He must have been napping, again, something else I hadn't noticed.

"Aspen, what have you done?" he roars, struggling to gain his balance. "Clean this up. Now."

I nod in response, walking carefully around the glass to the broom closet off the kitchen. The light above me flickers when I flip the switch, but nothing happens. Frustrated, I feel around for what I'm looking for, then stomp back to the kitchen.

When I return, my family is exactly where I left them, but instead of yelling or blaming me, they're all looking at the flickering sconces. They dim and brighten over and over again. Then, all at once, the lights go out.

CHAPTER 21

"*W*ell now look what you've done," Dallas grumbles, throwing a dishtowel at me. I catch it mid-air and bend, carefully pulling at the small shards of glass embedded beneath my skin. I then hold the rag against the oozing blood, applying pressure until I'm sure I won't bleed out on the floor.

I slap his arm roughly, scrunching my nose in disgust at his pigheaded attitude. "I didn't do this."

Even as I say the words, I'm not entirely convinced. I'd thought breaking the mirror would rid us of Ambrose, but what if...

Warmth trickles down my spine and the hairs on the back of my neck stand up.

"Oh hell," I whimper, closing my eyes as tears fill them. My empty stomach revolts and I clutch a hand over my mouth as the air around us sours.

I look across the counter at Mom, at the tears slipping down her face. My father is too busy flicking the light switches to notice, and my brother is in his own little universe blaming me for everything amiss in our lives.

"Mom, what's wrong?" Dallas reaches for her, noticing her expression, checking her up and down for cuts and bruises.

"Aspen," she trembles, reaching for me with unsteady hands.

I nod my head slowly, my own fear reflected in her glassy eyes. "You can see him."

Her chin jerks up and down in response, mouth forming the shape of a silent scream.

I didn't break Ambrose's hold. I set him free.

Clutching the broom, I turn full force into him, swinging it as hard as I can. The strong, knotted wood breaks against his skull, but he merely quirks his head to the side, smiling sickly and dragging his tongue across his decaying, rotted lips.

Ambrose yanks the broom from my hand, throwing it so hard into the kitchen cabinets that it shoots straight through the wood. Mom screams and Dallas yanks her down behind the counter for safety. My father reaches for me, but his intoxication is enough to send him tumbling into the couch, useless.

Ambrose latches on to my wrist and bends it backward, then clenches my hair in his fist. "You thought you could... get rid of me?"

Everything about him screams death, from his breath to his clothes and his touch. My dreams seem like a whimsical fantasy compared to the dank reality I'm facing. It's as if, where he touches me, a dark chill spreads across my skin and seeps into my veins until it reaches my heart, squeezing it between his bare hands.

His eyes darken, and he releases me for a split second before throwing me into the wall. Dallas charges at him, but

Ambrose sends him soaring into the granite countertop with a loud thud. My brother grabs his back, crumpling to the floor in pain.

"Mom, run!" I yell.

Her terrified eyes peek from behind the counter as I scream for her to save herself. She obeys, moving faster than I've ever seen her move. Ambrose doesn't seem at all concerned that she's got my father and is running out the front door, leaving behind both of their kids to a monster.

Ambrose assesses me with curiosity, clutching my neck and shoving my back into the wall before I have the chance to move. I push against his arms, beating on him, flailing, trying every move I ever learned at all those stupid self-defense classes I took to prepare myself for the next time I came face to face with Derek.

"My brother," I choke. "You made him crazy."

Ambrose shakes his head shortly, moving closer so I can feel his breath on my lips. "You cannot make a monster out of a good man. I only release temptation."

He snakes his hands up my sides and around my waist, grabbing at me and pulling at my clothes.

"You can't kill me," I cry, kicking at him with my battered shoes. "Your family needs me."

He shakes his head in disagreement and sweeps my legs out from beneath me, slamming my back flat on the hardwood. He moves so he's on top of me and brushes aside my long hair, then scrapes his tongue roughly against the veins in my neck.

"No. Please don't. Please," I cry, pounding on his chest, squirming as roughly as I can. "I'll give you my blood, just please—"

He pushes his palm hard into my ribs and a piercing crack

sounds throughout the room followed by my agonizing screams.

"It was you," I cough, spitting blood at his face, which he licks up greedily. "You killed all of those people."

His mouth forms a long thin line that peeks up in the corners, but I can't quite call it a smile. "Why were you protecting humans if you were the one killing them?"

This time his black teeth make an appearance when he smiles, and he moans wistfully. "There must be a balance."

Just keep him talking. Keep him talking.

"You saved people just so you could kill others?" I cry, gasping for air against the shooting pain in my side. Tears stream down my face, soaking my teeth. "And what about Emile, was that balanced?"

"Shut up," he growls, grabbing my jaw and tightening his hand around it threateningly. "She loved me. She wanted to be with me. I did her a favor." He releases me as his previous fury turns into a tortured memory. His hands roam down my skin and my clothes, feeling every crevice and curve of my body. "She couldn't love me like this."

I find it very hard to imagine who could, though I keep those thoughts to myself and pray he doesn't have mind-reading abilities along with his dream walker ones.

A clipping of Emile's death ended up with the rest of the ones from 1802—how is beyond my comprehension—and I came across her death date. December 12, 2019. He waited all those years so he could perfect the quintessential way for his true love to die. For some reason, it was important to Ambrose that even the numbers in the year add up to his signature pattern of twelves.

Whatever the reason, it made me realize something—I don't

think his spirit is just attached to the mirror, but connected to this house, as well. He's a part of it as much as the very structure that keeps it standing, which allowed him to control anyone that came near it, including Emile and the hunter who killed her.

"Why?" I croak against his tightening fingers, squeezing the very life from my body. His weight settles on me as his lips find the dip where my collarbone meets my throat, and he sinks his teeth in deep, pulling me to him with every gulp.

Just as my vision begins to blur, he pulls away, dragging out the process, savoring the taste of me on his tongue. I'm not sure if it's my blurred vision or the properties of my blood, but Ambrose's skin looks clearer and brighter somehow, as do his murderous eyes. His expression turns to one of scorn and hatred, instilling me with fear unlike anything I've ever experienced.

"Emile is the one who turned me in... after Elijah Troy told her he caught me. He wanted her to run but she did one better —do you like the name Troy? I thought it only fitting you go back to your roots. Anyway, she knew our clan would try to save me, so she never told them. Just the others. They said if I wanted to be a monster, I couldn't be a lamb, too. They cursed me so that my true nature would be all anyone ever saw of me, and that the unpredictable, dangerous true nature of any turned vampire after me would make them rash and uncontrollable. They used my actions to reign over our family with a lying cause. But that was for the three innocents I murdered to prove that as long as the Twelve were in charge, humans would continue to die by our hand. They cursed us to maintain control and scare anyone else who dared choose humanity over immortality. The others I killed were for...

something different. That's when they bound me here and took my soul."

"And you want to stop them. You want revenge." My mind is spiraling, trying to keep up with the twists and turns in his story that shatter everything I thought I knew about him.

Ambrose looks at me with intrigue. After Derek went mad, I had millions of internal conversations with myself consisting of what I could have said to talk him down, to reason with him. I had it all planned out, just a little too late to be of any use to him. Though maybe I still have a chance to change the outcome of this situation.

"You want them to suffer for what they've done to you and your family. Healing yourself isn't enough, Ambrose. You need an army. I can build you one." He can't know for sure the curse is broken until I fully turn. If he kills me now, he'll only be saving himself.

"You would do that?" He strokes my neck tenderly, releasing his grip on my throat just enough to give me some wiggle room.

I nod my head in assurance, taking his hand in mine as my other hand reaches out to the side. "I would turn for you."

My knuckles tighten around the wooden broom, and as fast as I can, I twist my body so that Ambrose loses his balance, then shove the wooden pole through his chest. He cries out in anguish as blood gushes from the gaping hole, running down his stomach to the floor, soaking into my clothes and splaying across my face.

If I'd had it my way, the way I envisioned every waking moment since the night my brother tried to murder everyone he ever loved, I would have killed him first.

I try to stand, but the persisting pains in my neck and side are too unbearable, so I crawl around the counter to where my brother's body lies still. I press my cheek to his chest but the blood rushing through my ears keeps me from hearing a heartbeat... if there is one.

"Aspen," Miles yells, bursting through the door so roughly I'm sure it's fallen from the hinges this time. He freezes, taking in the scene around him, the broken furniture, the blood on the walls, the blood on me. He rushes to my side, eyes barely noticing the lump on the floor that he once called family. His arms circle around my waist, making me suck in a sharp breath of pain where my ribs are cracked, if not broken. "What happened?"

"I broke the mirror." I drop my forehead against his chest, and he places a kiss atop my head. "I thought it would break his hold over us, but it set him free instead." Then my eyes travel back to my brother, and I decide everything else can wait until I'm sure he's alive. I try to move away from Miles, but he won't let me. "Dallas—is he?"

"He's alive. I can hear his heartbeat," Miles assures me, stroking my hair and my arms, checking me for more serious injuries.

"What took you so long?" I rub away the tears beneath my eyes only to realize my hand is covered in blood. I gasp, shoving it away from me so I can't see, so I don't have to look at it. Miles takes both of them into his own, supporting me until we're at the sink, where he grabs a handful of paper towels and douses them in warm water.

"Danielle is missing," he says, bringing back every ounce of the panic that was finally subsiding. He takes the wet towel and wipes it under my eyes, then gently across my cheeks. "We can't find her anywhere and Lucas is going out of his mind with worry. I was dealing with him while the rest of the family looked for her. I came as soon as I heard the 911 call from your mom."

"How did you—?"

"We intercept any calls that may be unexplainable to the humans. I've found we work faster than cops anyway."

I clutch my side but already the sharp stabbing has subsided some, probably a perk of my transitioning state. Miles pushes the hair off my shoulders and meets my eyes with his heavy stare. He tilts my neck back, putting aside the rag and dragging his tongue across the blood oozing from the holes in my neck. As he glides it slowly across my skin, the surface tingles where the wound was, and after a few moments, it's gone completely.

"Did you just?" I breathe, pressing my fingers to the smooth, unblemished skin.

He bites his lip, holding back a boasting smile. "Only your maker can heal you that way. I wasn't sure it would work since you're not a full vampire yet..." His eyes roam the area as the back of his hand trails over my scar, the one injury that hasn't healed since I changed, and I'm not quite sure why. Even the scar I have on my thigh from an old oven burn is completely gone, but not this one. Though, I get the feeling Miles is about to tell me why. "The bite that turns you never heals. It's sort of like a birthmark of your becoming."

For the rest of my life, I'll have a physical reminder of the day my life changed forever. The day Miles took a chance on a dying and broken girl, giving her more life than she'd ever had before.

"Did you drink the blood?" I ask, wondering how him tasting my addictive blood yet again is at all safe.

He surprises me by shaking his head. "I was about to when your mom called the police. I couldn't waste any time."

"Then how are you—" My words are cut off before I can finish asking how he's standing so close to me.

His mouth envelops mine hungrily and he grips my hips as if he's prepared to push me away at any moment. Our lips move in rhythm and my body conforms to him as I thread my fingers through his hair.

He grunts and pulls away from me before he loses himself, turning so I can't see the darkness that clouds over his golden eyes. I brush his chin with my fingers, indicating he can look at me, and he does so, tucking loose hair behind my ear and pressing his forehead to mine. "I realized there are worse things to be afraid of."

Miles walks over to my brother, but I can't bring myself to follow, unable to look at him like that for one more second because all I see is before... running into Derek and Rachel's room to find her crumpled on the floor in the most inhuman position I've ever seen, with Dallas lying beside her, still as a rock.

"He'll be okay." Miles turns away from me, rushing to the door.

"Please don't leave," I cry, then press my hands to my lips, unable to believe how helpless I sound.

Miles is in front of me within seconds, pulling me to his lips. "I'm not leaving, beautiful. You're coming with me."

He scoops me up in his arms and I curl against his chest with my hands covering my eyes. The longer they're open, the harder it is for me to pretend this isn't happening.

A groan sounds from behind us as my brother stirs. I can't let him wake up alone in a trashed and bloodied home, complete with an unknown dead body and his loved ones gone.

I open my mouth to speak, but Miles beats me to it. "Fine, but I'm not carrying him, too. He can walk." As I go to ask another question, he once again answers before I can get the words out. "Your parents are with Lucas. They're safe."

Before he can help my brother up, I grab his face, pulling his chin toward me and placing a kiss on his lips. "Thank you." I purse my lips, tears falling down my cheeks.

He kisses my nose tenderly.

"I told you." Bending, he helps my confused and sore brother to his feet, supporting his weight all the while cradling me in his arms. "There's nothing I wouldn't do for you."

CHAPTER 22

As soon as Dallas becomes aware enough to ask questions, I immediately regret bringing him along. He refuses to continue with us until we tell him what happened, but that is a much longer story for another day.

Dallas searches my face, then glances nervously up at Miles, who towers over him as much as he does me. "The man, where is he?"

"I killed him," I reply, which probably isn't the smartest choice of words, but at the moment, that's the least of my concerns. Keeping Dallas in the dark didn't protect him from Ambrose, so revealing the truth can't do that much more harm. The issue with telling him the truth is that he's bound to stick his nose where it doesn't belong.

"You—what?" he cries, shoving uselessly against the arm holding him captive. "Let me go!"

"Dallas." I reach for him and he extends his free arm, taking my hand in his, eyes wild with fear and hysteria. "I promise I will tell you everything, but you've been through enough for one night. Tomorrow morning, I'll explain it all."

I glance up at Miles, who doesn't look particularly happy about letting my brother, a human, in on his family's long kept secret. "I have to," I say so only he can hear.

He sighs, looking down at me in defeat. "I know you do."

"So, no more secrets?" Dallas pleads, waging me in a game I'd rather not play. I wasn't planning on telling him the whole truth. For example, that I'm on the verge of becoming a vampire and if I do that means I've killed a human being. If I ever complete the transition, I know it's the only thing he'll ever see when he looks at me, and I don't want that. I only know that because it'll be the only thing I see when I look in the mirror every morning. I'm not sure I'm capable of living with myself if I take a human life, but what's worse is my own brother looking at me and seeing a murderer. How long until the familiarity between myself and Derek is too much for him to handle? And what happens if the inevitable happens, and Miles can't protect me? Choosing humanity means I die, but choosing immortality means someone else must die for me to live. The transitioner state is my best option, but the reality of that choice is we don't know if it's survivable or not.

"No more secrets." I swallow hard, gnawing on my bottom lip anxiously. Desperate to change the topic to one that doesn't make me as anxious, I turn my attention to Miles, who's had his ears peeled the entire time we've been walking. He insisted we use human speed so he can listen in on the night in case it gives him any indication as to where his sister is.

"Do you think the hunters have Danielle?" I ask, earning a wide-eyed gape from my brother. He keeps his mouth shut though, trudging along.

Miles releases a heavy sigh, never removing his gaze from the depths beyond the tree-line. "They have to. No other vampires have crossed onto our territory, and there's no way this is the doing of one of our own. The clan still doesn't know about you."

"Are you sure?" I prod, knowing his unending faith in the clan can be blinding at times. Just as it was all those years ago when Ambrose committed murder. I have yet to tell Miles about that. I almost did, but decided that there's enough to worry about without adding age-old issues that are irrelevant to current events. We have more pressing matters at hand than an ancient vampire ghost who I believe I've just killed again.

Miles nods, and if he believes in them, then I suppose that will have to be enough for me... for now.

At the end of the day, they're not his family. Maybe I don't fully understand the clan dynamic yet, but I know people, and if there's a slight chance I'm the key to breaking their curse, I don't think Miles's affection for me will be enough to satisfy their hunger for justice.

"I'm sorry" —Dallas raises his hands, voice five octaves higher than it should be— "did you just say vampires?"

"No." Miles shakes his head, biting his lip in laughter.

"I could have sworn—"

"Dal? Tomorrow."

"Right," he breathes as we near Draven Manor. It's even more intimidating at night than during the day. The exterior lights shining up on the dark-stoned home cast shadows that seem to tower over the entire town. "Tomorrow. Tomorrow."

Vanesa storms out of the house, crazy with blind rage, charging toward us with vengeance in her eyes. "We have been looking everywhere for you. What were you thinking? Our sister goes missing and you and Lucas decide to disappear?"

"Is he back?" is all Miles asks, clearly thinking what I am—

they obviously didn't look everywhere if the first place they searched wasn't my house.

"Yes." Vanesa blinks her dark lashes rapidly, face red with fury. "With two humans. You need to let this sick fantasy go, Miles. You are in over your head."

"And you need to get out of yours." He shoves past her, indifferently.

I find it funny that she shares his strength and was unwilling to assist him with his baggage, i.e., my brother who's still struggling to break away. She eyes him with a look I'm not exactly comfortable with, taking him in with her soulless eyes, but I ignore it for now. The last thing I need is another reason to once again be the recipient of her rage.

Elliot opens the door with Vira behind, neither saying a word as they stop in front of us, both wearing stern, cold expressions.

Elliot eyes me with distaste and then spots my brother, who looks like he's about to pee himself. I suppose he's never been this close to Draven Manor, let alone on the front steps. "Another one? I think you've forgotten what we are, and it's not a concierge."

Vira moves between us and the doorway with eyes glowing dark in hatred. "Our little sister is missing and you gallivant off to save her? This pathetic excuse for a human who, might I remind you, came along just before all this started. How naive are you to think she has nothing to do with that?"

"Enough, Vira," Miles warns. He sets me down and I'm thankful—at least in front of his family, I want to look as if I can stand on my own, even if it feels like there's a fire burning in my lungs every time I breathe.

"Not nearly," she growls, getting in my face. "If anything

happens to Danielle..." Her gaze drags across Miles and to me, instilling a cold feeling deep in my gut. "I'll blame you."

Elliot shakes his head, undeniably sick of the bickering and finger pointing. He motions for my brother to follow him into the house, looking less than thrilled. Dallas turns, shooting me a look that asks whether or not I'll be okay. I give him a reassuring smile, knowing I'm safest with the Draven siblings no matter their biases against me, even if I don't trust them not to kill each other at times.

Miles moves slightly in front of me as if that could shield my frail, human body from his sister's wrath. It doesn't succeed in stopping her from getting as threateningly close to my face as possible.

Her vanilla-sweet perfume floods my senses as her ruby lips curl threateningly, teeth clenching with malice. "I will be your worst nightmare. I swear to God, princess, I'll—"

Vira's sentence falls short as an arrow sweeps through the air, squeezing dangerously between our shoulders and straight through Vira's middle. She clutches her stomach, falling back against the door with a thud.

Miles shoves me behind him, yanking his head around for the culprit. "Get in the house."

Vanesa joins us on the porch, squinting through the darkness for movement. Miles tries to shove me inside but I refuse to go without him. Whoever is out there was stealthy enough to get this close undetected, and I'd rather not give them the chance to pull anything else. It seems as if the hunters are more capable than the average human, and I'm not willing to bet anyone's life on that tonight.

"Get down!" Miles yells, but it's too late. A set of arrows fly through both Miles and Vanesa, splattering blood against the side of the house and all across my shirt, blending in with the dried blood already stained to the material.

Vanesa coughs, sending me a desperate look that actually makes me wish I could help her. She then falls to the side, off of the concrete porch and onto the muddy ground below.

I gasp, stepping backward and tripping on Vira's foot, scuffing up her black leather boots. If we survive this, she's going to murder me. Twice.

My hands reach for Miles as his eyes roll back in his head, and I grab him beneath his shoulders to break his fall, my legs taking the brunt of his weight.

It only halfway works because a pair of hands jolt me from behind. For a split second, I pray it's Elliot or Lucas until I feel a second pair yank me the rest of the distance onto the ground. The concrete does nothing to break my fall and my head slams against it so hard that keeping my eyes open is a strenuous task. I reach for the masked men with the pointy objects and commanding voices, but can do nothing but tug limply against the black fabric concealing one of their faces.

Darkness descends upon me as my eyelids close, and the surrounding world disappears.

CHAPTER 23

*D*amp grass soaks into my clothes as I struggle against the binds holding my hands behind me. Tight pains snake through my shoulders from the uncomfortable position, but I can't seem to find a more pleasant way to lie with my hands tied numbingly against my spine. I can't see anything besides the faint stars above and what looks to be a large flame flickering in the distance. There's quick movement all around, but I can't see from who or manage to get an approximation of how many. My gut says three, maybe four.

"Stop struggling," a deep voice commands, kicking me roughly in the side.

All right, better assume four.

I cry out, resulting in another kick, though this time I keep my mouth shut and focus on my breathing. In and out, in and out until the pain goes away. Mind over matter, Aspen, it only hurts as bad as you imagine it.

Those are words Derek used to preach to me as a child when he was teaching me to ride my bike. When I'd get a scrape or bruise I'd cry, no matter how bad, more afraid of harming myself than of the pain itself. He taught me to breathe away the hurt, counting in my head until it didn't sting so bad.

"Just like magic," he would say, then nudge my chin with his strong thumbs. "And now you get back up."

If only fear was so easily ignored. If only I could breathe this away until I've brought myself back from the brink of death. But it's not possible to breathe yourself back to life. The only thing you can do is breathe to keep yourself alive.

"You're not the Big Bad Wolf, Aspen. You can't blow down the obstacles in your way," Derek murmured in my ear when he found me crying in the bathroom my freshman year of high school, after my best friend ditched me for cooler girls who wanted to drink and smoke and meet boys. My plan was to punch her until she was sorry, but my ever-kind brother wasn't willing to watch me get suspended due to his long resonating advice.

A voice calls out from my left, and a clunking pair of boots walk in the direction of the sound. I take a deep, steadying breath, preparing myself for the worst but knowing I have to do something, and this could be my only chance. Arching my sore and tired back, I jolt my body to the right, rolling so I'm on my stomach. Beyond the large tree stump obstructing the bulk of my vision is a tall fire, surrounded by three posts, each with a person bound to it. I recognize the nearest one to me, slumped against the binds holding her upright.

"Danielle," I say beneath my breath, bile squirming in my gut and teasing my throat. I shimmy my body closer to the tree and shove my shoulder against it until I have a good enough grip to rise to my knees. The first thing I do once I'm sitting is attempt to get my hands in front of me, but I can't. Whatever's holding my wrists together refuses to budge. So not only am I helpless, but I'm helpless and without the only things that could possibly give me a fighting chance.

If the last hunter I came face to face with taught me anything, it's that I shouldn't count on them being slow. There's no way I'll manage to make a break for freedom. I double check my surroundings to reinforce my head count... two men stand off to the right, whispering anxiously with one another, who I assume to be the voice I heard prior and the man who kicked the wind out of me. Beyond them, closer to the fire, is another man who seems to have gotten the raw deal of keeping an eye on the vampires.

While scanning the other posts, I recognize Vanesa. She's unconscious just like Danielle and slumped in the mud with her legs bent beneath her.

A few feet away from her is Vira, but unlike her sisters, she's awake. She looks around horrified, eyeing her sisters and what looks to be another body slumped beside Vanesa, not bound at the wrists but still tied to the same post and unconscious.

I look away from their limp bodies, praying that they're okay, that they're not...

Closing my eyes, I take a slow breath. I don't even know it's Miles, even though it logically couldn't be anyone else. And if it is Miles, at least I know where he is.

"Vira," I call softly as possible, hoping the crackling of fire is loud enough so no one else can hear me. "Vira," I hiss, getting annoyed at her lack of attention. Now is not the time to wither in self-pity.

Her head lifts sharply and she turns her nose to the air, scouring the grounds for my voice. "It's me. To your right about fifty yards."

Puffs of smoke swirl through the air, tickling my throat and making me wish I at least had a sleeve to cough into or a way to get my shirt over my nose.

Vira's gaze locks with mine, panicked and rabid. All I know is if she breaks free from her restraints all hell will break loose. And frankly, that's the only plan I've got. "Are they alive?"

She nods once, keeping a close watch on the man guarding her family. He doesn't seem to have noticed she's awake yet, which would give her quite the advantage if she managed to cut the ropes keeping her tied to the post. Given she hasn't, I imagine they're coated in ash since I highly doubt this is the hunter's first time tying up vampires. I wouldn't take any chances either.

I start to inch closer, but she shakes her head quickly, nodding toward the two guards to my right. One of them is walking toward the fire which means his friend must be coming back for me. Her lips move in response, and I have to squint to make them out. The distance makes it hard to be sure, but it looks like she mouths, "Wait."

A sharp point pushes into my ribs before I have time to assess Vira's instruction. Wait for what? A signal?

"It's a shame to kill you." Hot breath bites into my ear. "But I think we both know you won't walk away like this never happened, will you?"

I fight against him as he brings me to my feet, shoving me in the direction of the others.

"If it weren't for you and your friends, I wouldn't be in this position in the first place," I spat, pulling against his hold.

As my captor goes to respond, his attention is drawn to the fire, where he calls out to another hunter. "Fletch, the thing on your left is awake."

This earns him a disapproving look from Vira, though the look could very well be aimed at me since she was doing just fine maintaining her cover before I started nagging her. The man shoves me onto my knees, holding a knife to my throat and slicing eagerly through the thin skin.

I glance up at Vira through my bleary eyes as the other man charges up to her, wooden stake in hand. I'd never gotten around to asking Miles what else kills a vampire. I always felt it was such a dangerous question to ask someone who constantly feels threatened.

I clench my jaw and close my eyes. I evaded death once before—I won't have another chance like that. This time the only people who can save me are facing the same fate.

There's a loud thud, and I open my eyes to see the guard shaking his head dizzily, charging at Vira once more. She bends her knees delicately before pushing off as her leg swings around, clocking the guy in the head. He moves closer to her and she locks her elbows to the pole, lifting both legs and clapping them over his ears. He grabs his head, falling backward toward the fire.

"Fletch, what are you doing?" the tall one yells from beyond us, charging toward them.

"Vincent didn't tell me she was an acrobat!" the attacker—Fletch—yells, climbing slowly to his feet.

The other man grunts, pausing ten feet away to decide whether or not his help is needed. "Just restrain her before the others get here."

Vira jumps, both feet flat against the wooden beam she's tied to, and walks herself up until she's at the top, then pushes off with all her might, soaring to the ground. She rolls once, shoving her legs through the restraints and managing to get her arms in front of her.

Why couldn't I be that cool?

The man stands just in time to meet her feet with his chest as she pounces, kicking him straight into the fire with bloodcurdling screams. The other hunter is now on her, two weapons in hand, and dodging every kick or punch she throws. It's clear to me now why the shorter man was the one keeping watch. He's expendable.

Vira's distraction gives me enough leeway with my own captor, and I shoot my leg backward, sweeping it beneath his feet so he falls on his back. The motion knocks me over, but I roll toward his head, bringing my heel down hard on his face, then scramble far enough away so I can stand without him grabbing hold of me.

"You bitch." He clutches his nose, lunging at me. Shooting pains run through my shoulders from the impact of my fall, but I manage to twist enough so the brunt of his body lands next to me. I knee his ribs with the sole purpose of teaching him how it feels, and rock to my feet, taking off around the fire.

"You think you can hurt me?" he grunts, grabbing a stone from nearby and throwing it at me. The object clocks me in the back of the head so hard, the world before me tilts and blurs until I'm not sure which way is up. "You're a human," he seethes, as if at some point between the beating and heavy objects pelting me in the head I'd forgotten. He catches up to me as I clamber to my feet, groping at the dirt beneath them. The fall knocked my bounds loose, so I at least have that going for me now. He latches onto my arm and yanks so hard that I go flying into Danielle's post. She stirs, but barely, fading in and out of consciousness quickly.

"So are you," I remind him, shoving a clump of dirt into his eyes and pressing my fingers into the sockets. He falls backward, digging at his eyes to rid them of the particles I hope are lodged so deep they'll need to be surgically removed. I run closer to the fire, closer to where Vira has just finished off the second hunter, looking a lot more worn than she had after disposing of the first. She retches into the grass, then wipes a hand across her sweaty forehead, swaying unsteadily on her heeled feet.

She's badly injured. From here it's hard to be sure whose blood is on her shirt, though from the amount of it, I'm praying it's not hers. She'll heal, but not fast enough to get everyone out of here on her own.

What if she can't muster enough strength to get rid of the last hunter? Or to heal me?

Vira looks up suddenly, taking a step in my direction. I squint, confused, and after a moment she stops, looking around at her fallen siblings as her decision takes root.

"I'm sorry," she mouths, turning her back on me. The hunter grabs me from behind and knocks my feet out from under me so I'm flat on the ground. His hand digs into the back of my neck.

"No," I say softly, struggling to find Vira through my watering eyes and the smoke-filled air. "Vira!" I cry out, screaming as he grabs my hair and buries my face in the dirt, muffling my protests. He grabs my arm and shoves it into the fire as I scream in agony, yanking it away and burying it beneath my chest, rocking back and forth.

"Not so consuming now, are they? You'd give your life for the very creatures that hunt your kind for sport." His voice elicits shivers throughout my body despite the sticky air and radiating heat from a fire that's three times my height. "It's sickening."

He yanks me onto my back by my hair and forces me to watch her as she attempts to untie her siblings with trembling fingers.

"You're no better, killing innocent vampires that haven't harmed anyone. They're not like the rest, they don't hurt people."

"Because they're cursed, and you're brainwashed. And we don't hunt them for sport, we hunt them for our survival. If we were not a prevalent issue, the clans would have no one to fight but each other, and that would be the end of the human race as we know it. The fewer vampires in the world, the better off we are." His reasonings would almost make sense if he wasn't trying to kill me.

If the hunters were so concerned with protecting humans, I wouldn't be here right now, fighting for my life. They'd have taken me in or tried to talk some sense into me, not blatantly attack me for simply wearing a necklace I found or kill me because I know too much about the vampires.

"Please don't kill me," I plead wholeheartedly, in hopes of bargaining with a lunatic. His fist tightens on my hair. "I will never be one of them."

"Yet, as long as you associate yourself with him, you will forever be attacked as if you are, and not just by us." The man squats beside me, something of compassion in his eyes, and I recognize for the first time that he's not a man, but a boy no more than my age. Possibly even younger. "I'm doing you a favor. You're already dead whether I kill you now or let you live."

He pulls out a knife, examining the rusted tip while I cradle my hand to my chest, tears streaming down my cheeks. My eyes zero in on the point that will end my life, and I realize it's not rust I see. It's dried blood. You don't stab a vampire with a silver knife—you use a wooden stake—which means this isn't the first time the hunters have killed a human that intercepted their agenda.

"I want to watch you kill her," I blurt, choking on the smoke from the fire. Fury erupts within me, and I use it to fuel my words. My chest aches with pain and anger, vision turning red. He looks down at me in confusion as if this is some kind of ploy. Taking his wrist, I latch my fingers around the blade of the knife, every nerve in my body on edge as I bring it closer to my throat. "Kill me after you kill her. She could have saved me but she didn't, and I'm going to die anyway. I refuse to go knowing the price of keeping her life was my death. She's already paid that toll. She's already taken a life in order to thrive for eternity. Please. That's my dying wish."

He assesses me carefully and his eyes bore into mine while he decides whether I'm genuine or not.

"Very well." He stands, but before he goes to Vira, he presses his boot to my throat, cutting off my airway. "If you try anything, I will make your death so painful you'll wish I burned you alive, understand?"

I nod my head, pushing against the weight of his large shoe, which is too thick to fit beneath my chin. He releases the pressure and holsters his knife, sneaking up behind the only conscious Draven. I don't see how he apprehends her in the midst of trying to find my balance. The farthest I can get to my feet are my knees, and that doesn't do me much good.

A fleeting thought repeats over and over again in my mind: *Run.*

There's a very small chance I'd get far, though. And what about my family? He'll never stop looking for me and won't be above hurting them to lure me out. The best chance I have of keeping them safe is Miles and his family.

I could let Vira die, though... that's a promising option, except I know the guilt would eat away at me for eternity, and dealing with her is a much easier price to pay.

I dip my arm in the cool puddle of mud to ease the burning before I begin dragging my limp body to where the hunter has Vira tied to a tree. He pulls something from his pocket and then smashes it in her face causing her to erupt in screams, shaking away the remnants sticking to her sweat. She fights and pulls at her restraints, but this time there's no way for her to get out. He must have caught her by surprise. Part of me hoped she'd hear him coming, but she must have been otherwise occupied with the fatal state of her siblings.

As I'm nearing the tree, I take three calming breaths so that my panicked wheezing won't give away my position. I grab a stick, rising shakily to my knees and aim for his head, but his hand shoots out, stopping me mid-swing just before I hit my target.

"Stupid girl." He kicks me from the side, hard enough to rattle my jaw, and I drop helplessly to the ground in defeat. I watch as Vira's blood drips onto my forehead.

Using my thumb, I wipe away the sticky substance and stare at it as he stabs her again with the wooden stake, as though he'd rather taunt his food before he eats it. This is more than a job for him. It almost seems... personal. He easily could have killed Vira right away, but he tied her up instead. Prolonging the torture.

A small part of me wishes she would bleed more so that I

could heal myself with her blood. Maybe then I'd have an advantage...

My eyes dart to the hunter's pant leg which has risen above his boot in our scuffle. As he's about to puncture one last hole into Vira, directly through her heart, I latch onto his ankle and sink my teeth deep into his skin.

CHAPTER 24

*B*lood soaks through my teeth and into my gums, warming my mouth as the liquid rolls smoothly down my throat, satisfying the hunger that's been lingering in me for days. Vira gasps above me and she stops struggling against her restraints. Everything fades besides the pulsing of his heartbeat as it grows fainter with each gulp I take. My own veins buzz with electricity, humming along with the sound of the blood being drained from his body, his entire life force being transferred into mine.

He tries to fight against me, attempting to yank his leg away and kick me with the other. But my grip on him is solid, and the longer I indulge, the stronger I become until I can hardly feel him hitting me at all.

When the beating of his heart ceases to lull me into a trance, I lick around the wound I've created, ensuring no drop goes to waste. Falling to my back, I watch as the small specks of light in the sky flicker in and out, enhancing and becoming more defined before blurring my vision altogether.

"It's like nothing you've ever felt before, right?" Vira's voice sounds so far away as she slides to the ground, resting her back against the tree as her blood pools around us. She doesn't seem to be in pain anymore. I think she'll survive her injuries, but either way, I'm not concerned at the moment as everything around me becomes more vibrant than it had when I began transitioning. It's as if I can see the energy and life radiating from every single thing around me, living or not.

And then reality sinks in, taking the place of the impenetrable high I felt only seconds ago; I killed a man. I mean, sure, he was going to kill me first, but that doesn't change what I did.

I rise to my knees, staring at the body before me. My eyes find Vira's as my words come out breathily. "I killed him."

"That would be the first thought you have after breaking the barrier between life and death," Vira says, annoyed that my inhuman state hasn't changed the direction of my moral compass. I think part of her hoped I would become someone Miles couldn't stand. "Now would you untie me before my bloody arms need amputated?"

After I untie Vira, I stand above my victim as she hunts for an animal to replenish her strength. Which, sadly, doesn't take her long.

"I take back everything I said before. I can't wait to drink from humans again," she informs me with her mouth full. I grimace and look away, not sure which sight is more gruesome.

"You have to burn him." She licks her teeth, tossing aside her meal. "A dead body holds evidence and raises questions. His identity could lead authorities to the other hunters, or to us. Leaving a crime scene also gives police a place to start. No one will think anything of the bonfire for a while, and by the time they do, the rain will have washed away the struggle."

"But his family?" I ask, staring at the boy before me. "They deserve to know."

"His name is Aaron Anderson. The whole town thinks he's in the military right now. Would you rather they spend their whole lives wondering if he's dead or alive, or wondering why there's no record of him ever being enrolled?"

"But if they think he's missing, they'll—"

"Do you think hunters are a group of burly men carrying knives and crossbows that get a high off of killing us? No. They're a strategic organization that has been in commission longer than I've been alive. They have strategies and ways of taking care of these sorts of things. They can't tell the police what really happened any more than we can."

I hate to admit it, but Vira's right. Finding his body will only lead to more questions. It could lead to us.

"Vira?" a voice calls. "Is that you?"

We turn to Danielle, and in an instant, I'm forgotten and Vira's at her sister's side, releasing her from her restraints. She holds her close as they collapse, rocking her sweetly back and forth. "It's all right, you're safe now."

While Vira comforts Danielle, I take the knife from the hunter's belt and finish cutting Vanesa and Miles loose, careful not to let Vanesa land face-first on the concrete. She moans, looking up at my face foggily.

"You're not human," is all she says before her eyes lull back in her head. The fire is dying swiftly, which means ash is beginning to cool around it, weakening us all. Being this near to it makes me feel as if I'm dying of dehydration and my skin is turning itself inside out over and over again. I'm not sure how Miles managed to stand it for so long.

"Miles." I lean over his body, tucking away the loose hairs that have fallen onto his face. I pat his cheek until his eyes begin moving under the lids. "Miles, wake up."

Police sirens sound from far away, echoing through the town. We don't have much time.

"Who called the police?" Panic settles in my chest as I struggle to keep Miles awake. Vira doesn't answer, and I'm surprised when a light weight drapes over me instead.

"Aspen." Danielle lunges, wrapping me in a hug so tight I can hardly breathe. "Thank you. And... welcome to the family."

"Thanks," I say unsteadily, tossing a loose arm around her shoulders.

"We have to go," Vira says. "Can you get Miles? We've got Vanesa. The police are about ten minutes out."

I look around, realizing I don't see any flashing lights. I could have sworn they were right on top of us.

"You'll get used to it." Danielle reads my mind, smiling knowingly. "Judging distance is harder when everything sounds so loud."

Danielle picks up Vanesa, draping one of her arms across Vira's shoulder and one across her own. Before they leave, Vira looks back at me, giving Vanesa to Danielle and instructing her to keep walking.

Once Danielle is a safe distance away, Vira clears her throat, looking around uncomfortably. "What you did for me... I don't take that lightly. I know how badly you wanted to stay human. I know you never wanted this life."

I nod my head once, and in a flash, she's gone as if the wind swept her away.

I think that's the closest thing to a thank you I'm going to get from Vira Draven.

Miles's hand reaches out to mine, and I'm relieved to see his eyes are open and alert again. He stares at me melodically, then props himself up on shaky elbows.

"How does it feel?" His voice sounds dry and raspy like he just woke up from a long nap.

I bite my lip, smiling nervously as my hands quiver against his face. "Terrifying. Invigorating."

The sky lights up just beyond the center of town, which gets us moving quickly, throwing the ropes in the fire and limping toward the edge of the trees.

"The body." I halfway turn and point toward the hunter lying in the center of the clearing. Miles shakes his head, ushering me into the thick trees where we won't be seen. If we run through town now, we risk being seen by the police or curious eyes peeking through their blinds.

"Stay in the car," an officer orders someone, as he and another walk onto the scene, shining flashlights across the landscape.

"There were a lot more people here than just him." The other officer notices, pointing his beam at the body, and then at the scuffle around him.

We duck behind a tree to ensure we're not seen, and when I lean forward to look, Miles touches my arm gently. With an urgency in his voice, he says, "We should go."

I press my hand to his chest before he can whisk me away, which was a lot easier when I didn't have strength of my own to fight against him.

Moments later, I hear another door open, followed by a meek voice. "It's him, isn't it? Where is he?"

"Dammit, Martin, what are we paying you for?" one of the cops grunts as the other struggles to hold the girl back.

Suddenly, she lets out a scream that makes my ears ring, feet pounding to the site of the body. Miles tugs at me again but I shush him, wanting to see what happens, wanting to know why the girl is here.

I peek tentatively beyond the tree as my heart sinks, watching her drop down next to the man who will be labeled a tragic victim in the days to come. "No. No, oh my God, no. Aaron. Baby, no."

Miles drops his face into my neck, holding my hands to his chest as my legs go numb. My whole body feels stiff and foreign, as if I don't belong in it anymore. "They were—?"

He nods into me, squeezing me around the waist. "That's Nadia Porter."

"Did she know?" I force my tongue to work despite the heavy weight holding it down.

"No. She thought he was—"

"In the military," I finish, releasing a shuddering breath. "That's why you wanted to leave so badly."

"Come on. Let's go check on your brother," he says instead, avoiding my question. This time I allow him to pull me away. I look back though, watching the poor girl cry over the body of her dead lover while the police try to pry his cold, dead skin from her fingers. I notice a beautiful ring glistening off one of them.

Now she will spend the rest of her life wondering what really happened to her fiancé and why he lied to her. So many scenarios will run rampant through her mind before she can process the truth that will inevitably make her hate him for not loving her enough to tell her the truth. She'll blame him instead of the one who took him from her. The memories she held dear will fade over time, replaced with the dark, repressing sadness accompanied by hearing his name or seeing old photographs of the two of them when she believed so wholeheartedly that they were happy.

That is, after all, what I did with my brother.

CHAPTER 25

*E*ight of us sit in a semicircle inside of the house Miles first brought me to after I turned. We're mostly silent, minus Vanesa who has continuously been spouting off orders and worst-case scenarios, which at the moment is no help to anyone but her own restless mind.

"She needs to turn someone," Vanesa argues, pacing the floor like a maniac. "That's the only way to know whether or not the curse has been broken. Does anyone... I don't know, feel any different?"

Lucas pokes Danielle in the arm, then looks to Vanesa with a taunting grin. "Hmm, no, Dani feels normal. Anyone else?"

She swats his hand away as Vanesa stops pacing, pointing a long, slender finger in his direction. "Need I remind you of your absence the past half an hour? We could have died and you wouldn't have known the difference!"

"Vanesa, we scoured the entire freaking town looking for you! The hunters must have cloaked your location or something to keep us away!" Lucas argues, shooting to his feet.

"Is that supposed to—"

"I think we're best to focus on what lies ahead, not behind," Elliot interrupts, pinching the bridge of his nose as if he's in pain. "This is getting us nowhere."

Vira takes Vanesa's hand and pulls her so she's resting on the edge of the couch. "I think what Vanesa is trying to say is we would be dead had Aspen not been there. And I'm not kidding, so roll your eyes, call us dramatic, but it's true. If Aspen hadn't gotten in his head, he would have killed her, then me, then the rest of us, and come for you next."

"She has a point," Danielle speaks up and Lucas takes her hand, suddenly more serious about the matter. The two of them are close, and given that they're not true family, I get the impression their bond goes deeper than that of a brother, sister relationship. "I may not have been awake, but we were all grabbed from our own property. The humans in town don't dare stray this far. Not even the young kids who deem themselves the bravest by getting the closest."

"They're getting cocky," Elliot agrees as Lucas adds, "They're planning to wipe us out completely."

"Which brings me back to why Aspen needs to turn a human. Then we can double the size of our clan and they won't have a fighting chance. I won't risk it if it doesn't work for her, but we need the numbers." Vanesa tries to stand again, but Vira holds her down.

"It'll work," Miles says from the fireplace—electric, of course. Much like Elliot, he looks about done with this discussion. We've all had a terribly long night and Vanesa continues to make life-altering decisions a priority over rest.

Just like before, it's as if they're making my choices for me and I don't appreciate it. I refused to turn because I didn't want to harm a human, and though circumstances changed, I'm still not okay with turning an innocent as a test dummy. I won't turn someone who doesn't choose it first.

"I'm sorry, my sister has to what now?" Dallas sits on the couch between Elliot and Vira, still as a board. But even scared stiff, he can't keep his mouth shut.

"Why the hell is he here again?" Vanesa snaps, then bites her tongue once she realizes he's scared out of his wits and her talking about him like he's not in the room isn't helping the situation any.

"He's Aspen's brother, and he's not safe anywhere else." Danielle rolls her eyes, fiddling with her royal blue heart pendant.

"You've sure become vocal since being kidnapped," Vanesa quips, tossing her hair over her shoulders, this time breaking free from Vira's hold, who drops her head in defeat. She looks around at her brothers, but none of them make a move to assist. Miles doesn't seem to be in the same conversation as the rest of us, let alone prepared to intervene in case of a disastrous event.

Danielle stands, measuring up to her older, and much taller, sister. "Vanesa, maybe I'm just sick of you deciding for the rest of us. In case you have forgotten, you're not the oldest and people still have a choice."

"Fine. Okay. Let's take a vote." Vanesa smiles eagerly, looking around the room at her less-than-enthused siblings. "Who here thinks Aspen needs to turn someone so we can finally get on with our lives?"

"You weren't so eager to end the curse when I was still human and you didn't believe it would work," I point out and regret it immediately.

"I wasn't asking you," she says bitterly, turning back to her real family. "You know what, no. Give me one good reason why you won't turn someone, other than innocent human souls and your moral bullshit."

What the hunter said resonates with me, and since I took his life, I think it's only appropriate that I take into consideration what he said, because other than his intent to kill me, he wasn't all crazy in his reasoning. "How many people have to die to become like you? To fill your army? How many innocent humans will die in a turf war with the other clans once you're strong enough? Sides will be chosen, and the human race will get caught in the crossfire. Tell me I'm wrong."

Elliot stands, looking around at each of his siblings and then at me. "You're not human anymore, you need to stop thinking in their favor. I'm with Vanesa."

After he announces his stance, which I fear holds weight with the others, he exits the room without another glance. Vanesa looks all too pleased with her brother's decision, and I hold my tongue to keep from getting my head bit off.

Miles walks around the couch and rests a hand on my shoulder, backing me one hundred percent.

"You all know where I stand," he says, then sits beside me, placing a kiss on my cheek affectionately. At least I know he has my best interest at heart.

One thing I respect about Miles is his ability to put others' needs before his own. He understands who he is—or more appropriately, what he is and where he stands. Regardless of how long it's been, every vampire in the world was once human, yet it seems to be a trait they bury within themselves. Miles never has, even after all these years. I respect him for that. As demonstrated here, not everyone is willing to see the side opposite of what they want.

"Big surprise." Vanesa rolls her eyes. "Next."

"I'm with Danielle and Miles." Lucas shrugs, which honestly surprises me considering he hasn't exactly been supportive. "I'm sorry I didn't have faith in you from the beginning, Aspen. I promise that will change." Lucas reaches across Danielle to rest a hand on my knee. "We've sustained ourselves for long enough that I think we've proven our family is all we need. You are part of that now."

At this, Danielle smiles, looking at him with delight, then up at Vanesa's disapproving expression, turned-down lips, and furrowed brow.

Vanesa moves her glare to Vira, who could either tie the votes or tip the scale since I don't have a say and my poor brother is looking lost as a doe-eyed puppy who strayed too far from home.

Vira meets my eyes, searching for something within them I'm not sure of, then closes her own while breathing a heavy sigh. "She doesn't have to turn anyone if she doesn't want to, Vanesa. I think we need to break the curse, but ultimately it's her choice and we can't force her." She stands, reaching for her sister in apology.

Vanesa pulls away, but Vira's too fast, stopping her in her tracks before she can storm off. "Don't do anything stupid."

Her warning makes me uneasy. And here I thought Vira was always the flight risk.

I stand as well so I'm level with Vanesa, though her heels give her a few inches on me. "Then it's settled."

Her eyes glow red, and in an instant, she's gone.

"I think we could all use some rest," Vira announces, stretching her arms.

Before she can leave though, I call after her unsurely,

knowing I need to ask so I don't drive myself crazy. She was willing to leave me for dead not an hour ago. So I don't know why she's so concerned with giving me a now. "Why?"

Her eyes scan me mindlessly as she bites her lip in thought. Her dark hair is messy and knotted with blood as I'm sure mine is. She looks like death. "You saved my life, and by extension, my family's. I owe you a lot more than a choice."

It's obvious Vira is trying her best to be sincere, but it's not a trait that comes easily to her. If she ever figures out I'm the one who scuffed her shoes, I don't think she'll be as humbling and grateful.

"You were going to leave me there," I blurt, despite our unspoken agreement to never bring it up again. I can't ignore my need to know how she could change her opinion of me so quickly.

Vira shoots a nervous glance at Miles before answering. I bet she hoped he would never find out she could have saved me and didn't. She could have ended the fight long before I killed a man.

"There's nothing I put before my family," she says sternly, nodding at her brother. "Including their own wishes."

Danielle and Lucas trail behind her, but Danielle stops when he exits the room, facing me with an earnest expression. "They didn't let me choose. I was the youngest, so they all turned before I was old enough to pass for an adult if need be. But I chose humanity until I found something I couldn't live without. Lucas was already a vampire when he came to us, in need of a home and training, much like Emile was. I had been willing to grow old while my siblings stayed frozen in time, but my family ensured I could never make that decision. Your choice to turn was taken away from you a lot like mine was, and I just want you to be sure when you make your next one. Because in the end, you'll have to live with the consequences of that decision."

And with those words of wisdom from a two-hundred-year-old fifteen-year-old, I'm left feeling a little speechless as she ducks out of the room.

"You know, I used to find vampire films enthralling."

"And now?" Miles drops his chin to my shoulder, playing with the ends of my hair which are much more vibrant now than they were before my transition.

"Not at all," I sigh, falling back into him.

Dallas watches us with dismay, and I hate myself for once again forgetting he's in the room. When Vira, Vanesa, and Danielle left us at the fire, they went straight to Miles's hideaway, stationed deep in the woods. They called Lucas and Elliot over, who brought Dallas along with my insistence. My parents are safely tucked away at home and supposedly won't remember a thing. I'm not entirely sure how that works given they don't have their compulsion back yet, but I've learned not to ask questions… okay, that's a lie. I ask way too many questions, but Elliot refused to tell me what he did, so I gave up. That's a fight for another day.

"Are you sorry you turned?" Miles asks, placing a kiss on my scar. The rest of my wounds have healed, including the burns on my arm, but as Miles predicted, my maker's mark has yet to disappear.

I tilt my chin so his lips can meet mine, soft and light. "I'm just sorry it took me so long."

"Does anyone care that I'm freaking out?" Dallas interrupts, looking a little worse for wear. His hair is greasy from the amount of times he must have run his fingers through it, and his leg is moving in constant vibration, a side effect of his nerves. There's a small, lopsided bruise forming an outline around his cheekbone, which I assume to be an injury from his run-in with Ambrose. Danielle gave him something for the pain in his back, but I don't expect it to heal nicely.

I purse my lips, unsure of how to make this okay for him. Much like him, I was thrown into the middle of this crazy world, but the difference is, I felt the change because it was happening to me. It was hard for me to deny the truth when I was living proof of it. Dallas, on the other hand, is on the outside looking in at a world he only believed to be true on television screens and in movie theaters.

"Dallas, I know you've heard some crazy things tonight but—"

"Crazy doesn't begin to cover it, Aspen. We've only been here a few weeks and you've managed to get yourself mixed up in-in I don't know what." His wide expression searches mine for answers he can't begin to comprehend. "How long has this been going on?"

"Promise to keep an open mind?" I ask, leaning forward and feeling Miles's hand rest on my lower back for support.

"I'm not promising anything."

Fighting the urge to run and leave Miles to clean up our mess, I rip the bandage off to save both me and my brother the extra pain of drawing this out. "It started this week. The night I never came back? I was attacked by a man in town, and I kind of… died. The Dravens are vampires and Miles turned me to save my life."

Dallas stares at me, slack-jawed and dumbfounded for a solid minute until the vein in his forehead tics in irritation. "Do you think I'm an idiot?"

"I'm serious, Dallas, vampires are real."

"Yeah," he scoffs. "And in the woods, I got bit by a dog and am suddenly a wee bit hairier."

Miles chooses now to speak up, though his response doesn't help me much. "Not possible, we drove werewolves to extinction hundreds of years ago."

Dallas gives Miles an exasperated look, as I say, "He was kidding." Then to Dallas, "Please take this seriously. You wanted the truth, it's not my problem if you don't believe it."

"These vampires. You're one of them?" Dallas stands, looking at me closely. "You're a little paler than before, but that's about it."

I blink rapidly, swatting his hand away. "You recognized the man that attacked us, right? The one from your painting?"

His face goes still, not a drop of color left in his already pale complexion. "I thought I was seeing things."

"You weren't. Those nightmares I was having... they were of him. He caused them and taunted me."

Dallas releases a shaky breath, settling back on the couch and resting his eyes. "I knew him when I saw him, I just didn't want to believe it... he'd been in my dreams, too, only a few times, though, when I napped in the study. That must be why I was so quick to dismiss yours. He would... talk to me... tell me stories. Honestly, I think he wanted someone to listen to him, but it weirded me out. He told me everything, but every time I woke up, I wouldn't remember until I slept again, or painted— sometimes I'd get flashes of him then."

Miles leans forward, intrigued. "Subconsciously, he's known all along. Ambrose must have repressed the memories somehow, but now that he's dead, he no longer holds control."

Or maybe my brother can think for himself again now that he's away from that soul-sucking house.

"How was Ambrose able to do all of that?" I wonder aloud. Dallas seems to have checked out of the conversation, delving into his own webbed mind to distinguish fiction from fact, the line that separates the two now much, much thinner.

Miles shakes his head. "It exceeds any vampire capabilities recorded in history. How he managed to stay here beyond life is a mystery to me, but as for his powers, he did have two hundred odd years to perfect them."

"I suppose you're right." I bite my lip, hoping he's gone for good this time. I mean, can you even kill something that isn't alive?

Miles brushes his lips across my knuckles. "What are you going to do now?"

CHAPTER 26

*M*y heels click down the long, white hall, each door the same as the next the whole way down. It's mostly vacant, as I figured it would be at this time of night, which is exactly why I waited. A few people in lab coats roam about but pay me no attention, thanks to the visitor's pass I swiped on my way in.

I'm a vampire now, I don't have to abide by the rules... or at least, that's what I've been telling myself. Truthfully, I feel so dirty having stolen and broken into a sealed wing of an assisted living center, but it's necessary and I can't let my conscience get in the way of everything.

Room 224 lies ahead on the left, and I double check my surroundings before letting myself in with my—also stolen—key card. The card reader beeps twice, switching from red to green, and I peer around one last time before slipping inside.

A young girl sleeps in the bed in front of me, light brown hair splayed across the snowy pillow. Dozens of roses and get-well cards sit at her bedside, the only splash of color in an otherwise dull room, lacking any sense of personality. If it weren't for the duffle bags of well-worn clothes, I'd think she was only here for the weekend. It's been a year. An entire year of doctors' appointments and pain medications so strong, she's lucky not to have developed an addiction. Because unlike most, she's one of the unlucky few who still feel the pain.

As the fluorescent lights cast my shadow over her, her eyes open drowsily, and she takes in my appearance. She reaches for me, and I take her hand as she touches my face in awe. Then reality crashes in, and she pulls it away, clutching it to her chest in fear. She reaches for the panic button, but I block her, ripping the attachment from the bed.

"What do you want?" Her bottom lip quivers while she tries to hold back her tears.

I purse my lips, stepping away from her with my hands up, easing down onto the visitor's chair. She seems more relaxed knowing I'm farther away.

"My brother ruined your life," I whisper, eyeing her as my memories of her full-of-life, round, electric eyes are replaced with this new image of the hollow shell of a girl who lost her life to a man that didn't love her enough to cling to reality.

"You never came to see me. Your parents tried, but never your brother. Never you." A tear runs down her face and she wipes it away fiercely. "Why?"

"My parents—they said you didn't want to see us," I reply, wiping a tear of my own away. Rachel was once my idol, the person I wanted to be most like in life. I wanted to be as courageous as she seemed, and now she looks small and helpless, sunken into a bed so worn from her body it envelops her like a cocoon.

"I didn't want to see them. But I wanted to see you, Destiny. A sister's bond can never be broken."

I smile at those words, my chest swelling with love and hate and pain. Hearing her refer to me as my old self releases feelings and memories I've long since buried. I'd always wanted a sister, and the day Rachel first called me hers was the highlight of my life. I remember feeling grown up at fifteen, bold and fearless because I was part of Rachel's life. And not just her life, but her family, her world. "I want to help you."

"Unless you can give me my legs back, it's a little too late for that," she scoffs, rolling her head so all she can see is the ceiling. I suppose that's the only view she has, the blank and lifeless walls. Meanwhile, I get to see the world in a whole new light. I get to experience things in a way I never have before, and it's thrilling. It just doesn't seem fair. Rachel deserves so much more than an empty, lonely bedroom.

I find myself staring at the place where her nose ring used to be, the golden hoop she never took out—her signature look. It's gone, along with everything else recognizable about the girl I used to know. "What if I could?"

She rolls her eyes, smiling bitterly as her head snaps in my direction. "That's not funny."

"I'm serious." I lean forward and she moves as far from me as possible, which in her state isn't much. I'm scaring her, which was not at all my intention. "Hypothetically, if I could get you your legs back, no matter the cost, would you want them?"

"Your brother took everything from me. My parents can't bear to visit anymore because they hate seeing me in pain. They send flowers now, instead. One time my little sister came in and saw all the mangled tubes sticking out of me. She's terrified now. I haven't seen her in eight months. You do the math. I would do anything to get my life back."

"Are you sure?" I stare into her eyes, and she begins to look more uneasy than before, eyeing me up and down as if searching for some sort of resemblance to my brother.

Her expression slacks when she finally comes to a conclusion. "You're not kidding."

I shake my head in response.

"Close your eyes." I place my hand on hers, and this time she lets me. "Do it," I insist when she continues to stare blankly.

I pull her wrist to my mouth, taking an unsteady breath. She does as I say, keeping her eyes closed, but I can feel her trembling, her heartbeat speeding up. Rachel thinks I'm going to finish what my brother started. That I'm going to kill her.

A breath escapes her lips as my teeth pierce the skin that blocks my venom from her veins, and it's only a moment before the fluid is humming through her body.

"What are you doing to me?" She shakes rapidly, struggling against my hold. She tries to yank her wrist away, which only makes me latch on tighter. When her arm finally goes limp, I release my hold, placing her arm across her stomach. She looks up at me, higher than any of her medications could make her. "My legs are... tingling." She gasps, movement from under the blanket widening her eyes. "I can feel my toes. How did you..."

"I'm a—" I pause, deciding against the outright truth. After Elaine and Dallas, I promised myself the next time I did this I would practice using subtlety a little more. Except, I don't have the time to ease her into this before someone from the American clan discovers I'm here. She's safer on her own for now. "I'm a vampire. To complete the transition, you have to drain a human life to keep the balance."

"Why?" she breathes, shifting herself up higher on the large pillow beneath her head.

"If it weren't for my family, you'd still have one." I smile sadly, moving toward the door. "They can never know," I add, and she nods mechanically. They'll have too many questions neither she nor her doctors could ever answer. "You have to disappear, Rachel."

"You're crazy," she accuses halfheartedly, staring fearfully at the two parallel holes on her wrist where blood pools and spills down her caramel skin.

"You know I'm not. You can feel it."

"You're just going to leave me like this?" Her eyes grow wide, and she uses her slowly strengthening arms to sit up even more.

I nod once, listening to the echoing footsteps a few doors down. I have approximately two minutes until they reach this hallway and find me where I'm not supposed to be. "I can't stay. It's not safe for me to be here or for us to be seen together. You will find me when you're ready."

She breathes heavily, frantically looking around the room through squinted eyes. I'm almost through the door when she stops me in my tracks, sending icy shivers down my spine.

"You know the first thing I'm going to do, right?" she calls.

"I'm just giving you back what he stole. What you do with it is entirely up to you." I grab the door handle at the last second before it snaps shut, peering through the opening for one final thought. "Oh, and give him my best, will you?"

Elaine stands nervously, eyeing the staff around the empty waiting room. "I told you, you could have waited in the car."

She rolls her eyes in annoyance. "Yes, yes, I could have

waited in the car. I could have waited at the airport, I could have waited at home. Aspen, I'm the watcher. Watching is my job and you're the only Draven member who is unbeknownst to the rest of the world."

"Are you even sure the other eleven clans care that much?" I question, wondering what makes the Draven family so threatening, besides the obvious.

Elaine unlocks the car, opening the passenger door for herself. "You broke the curse. That makes you more powerful than any other human or vampire on this earth, past or present, as far as we know. Vampires aren't known to turn on their own kind, so this whole mess is unprecedented."

My spine tingles, and I sense someone watching us from behind. A man, I think. He seems old—much older than the Dravens—and radiates the sort of darkness that makes my skin crawl.

"You're right, get in the car." I shove Elaine into the seat, preparing to close the door on her straggling leg if she doesn't lift it fast enough.

"Are you just trying to shut me up?" she accuses, trying to wrestle with me and failing miserably.

I push her inside, closing and locking the doors so she can't get out, or more accurately, so he can't get in.

"What do you want?" I turn with purpose to find a tall, pale man standing beyond the car, eyeing me with suspicion.

He tsks, peeking gingerly in the car at Elaine before returning his unwanted attention to me. "Brave. I was intrigued to learn there was an undocumented vampire in my territory."

"I'm sorry, did I need to sign some sort of waiver?" His

eyebrows raise at my boldness, and he takes a step in my direction.

The clouds seem to haze over, swallowing the sun as he lowers his neck. He breathes in deeply, eyes growing dark. "You've come from Ichorye."

"I was just passing through. Visiting some old friends." I keep my responses simple like Miles and I practiced before I left, in the event I ran into another of our kind.

"The Dravens don't have friends." The man sneers, not for a moment believing my cover story. He must smell them on me.

I swallow the fear creeping up my throat and take a step toward him. "Yes, well, I was an old friend of Ambrose Draven. I heard some odd years ago from a friend of a friend that he'd died, and I guess I was just hoping the rumors were true."

He completely ignores my well-rehearsed explanation and continues on with his accusations. "I wasn't aware the Dravens had any other members."

I focus on breathing evenly and keeping my heartbeat from building up. "Neither were they. He mustn't have told them since I was one of his massacres, or so I assume. I left before even I knew what I was, much less them."

"That must have come as much of a… surprise."

"Indeed. Now if you'll excuse me, I must be on my way."

"You smell new," he says, unmoving as I round the car.

I smile forcefully, looking to the ground as if I'm bashful. "Don't flatter me. I believe my heart's taken by another."

Without another word, I turn the ignition and drive away from the parking lot as casually as possible, and when I look back, he's nowhere to be found.

"Who was that?" Elaine whispers, turning in her seat to snag a glimpse of yet another mysterious vampire. "And are they all so hot?"

"A problem." I grab my seatbelt, fastening it now that we're far enough away that I feel safe. Elaine looks at me with questioning eyes, then places her phone in my extended hand.

"Already in trouble?" Miles answers, a smile in his voice.

"What can you tell me about an American vampire, tall, blonde, pasty." I skip the pleasantries.

Elaine muffles a laugh with her fist, grinning out the window.

"I'm afraid you will need to be more specific," Miles sighs, and I feel a little guilty for describing half of the vampire population.

"He has a tattoo behind his ear. Like a circle. I couldn't tell, I was too busy feeding him lies." Miles goes quiet at once. "What?"

"Adrian. He rules most American territories. If he came to you himself, then people are talking. He's interested. More importantly, he's on to us. Who was with him? We need to know how many are aware of your existence."

"He came alone. No protection," I tell him, swerving through lanes of traffic so we don't miss our flight. Finding Rachel proved to be more difficult than I'd thought.

"He wanted to scope out the unknown variable on his own." Miles pauses, taking a deep breath of relief. At least this means the whole country isn't looking for me. "Whatever you do, be careful, Aspen. You've got his attention now and he's not someone to mess with."

"We'll be fine. I promise."

"If you doubt that even for a second, you call me and I'll be there," he swears, and my chest swells at the sentiment.

If Adrian wanted to hurt me, he wouldn't have let me leave. Besides, Miles coming here would only arouse more suspicion. Even so... I don't have the heart to refuse him. "I will."

"Be safe," he whispers, then hangs up.

Elaine manages to keep quiet for a mere five minutes before bombarding me with conversation. I've begun to realize she doesn't do well with silence, which is mostly what I'd prefer. "Did you tell Miles your theory?"

"He doesn't believe me," I say, knowing from the start what would happen when she first came to me with the information.

"What about the Wicked Witch?"

"I didn't tell Vira." I laugh at her choice of names. "She doesn't even know I'm here trying to test the curse, and from the looks of it, it's broken. Besides, what does it matter? It doesn't change what's happened."

Elaine falls quiet again, though I'm not naive enough to think it will last. In the meantime, I allow my thoughts to wander to my theory of Ambrose and the curse. When I first explained to Elaine how I turned and what I discovered about Ambrose Draven, she showed me her ancestor's journal, which talked in detail about everything revolving around the Draven clan, given he was their watcher, after all. The journal was spelled so only members of the Graves family had the ability to read the secrets kept within its bounds, though Elaine figured out a way to give me temporary access. Something involving dead animal blood—I don't know, nor do I want to. As it turns out, there are twelve major vampire clans across the world. A few smaller clans fall beneath them but ultimately the Twelve— the leaders that reign over them—control everything that happens as well as the laws made. When their father died, Ambrose and his brother—Miles's dad—Edgar, were the contending replacements. The remaining clan members chose Edgar despite Ambrose being older and the rightful chairman.

This is what started his downward spiral. Ambrose was desperate to regain the respect he thought he deserved and was angry with the clans for choosing his brother simply so he wouldn't wield as much power with their followers. The Twelve wanted to eat freely and kill freely, and Ambrose was making a convincing argument as to why they shouldn't kill without purpose. That's when I believe Ambrose violently killed three people, desperate to frame the council and take back his influence. But when Emile turned him in, they kept the truth hidden and used him as an example of why one should never challenge them.

When the clans cursed him, the members drew from the Twelve's power, and my theory is that the number has something to do with breaking the curse. I think Ambrose figured it out. It's very possible I still would have been the way to break it, considering I was able to turn—and it can't be a coincidence that my ancestor fled London after turning Ambrose in. He must have known our bloodline would be a key ingredient—but I believe Ambrose discovered a different way, one that would bring him back after death. That's why he needed me.

One death every twelve days, which he never got to finish before the clans caught on. He only managed ten. Then Emile being the eleventh death happened on the twelfth of December 2019. And finally, me. My blood was meant to heal him, not break the curse as he claimed. My death, on the other hand, being the twelfth and final, might have done the trick. The day he attacked me was the twelfth of July, and that date can't be a coincidence. It's possible draining my blood and my life force may have brought him back.

My ancestor held the key to breaking the curse, and it was passed down through the generations to me. Maybe Ambrose figured out another way, to not just help his family, but to free himself by completing his sacrifices and using me as the final ingredient to bring him back to life.

Maybe there were multiple ways, or maybe I've given these possibilities too much thought and am just rambling nonsense, but I can't help wondering if there was more to it.

No matter the true release, I was a casualty either way.

CHAPTER 27

*E*laine and I cautiously board the plane back to London, keeping a close eye out for anyone that looks suspicious or like the living dead. I don't particularly like that term, but she claims it's a fairly accurate description of those who have died and still continue as functioning members of society.

"Do you think we were followed?" she asks once we're safely tucked into a cab, twenty-five minutes from home. Miles wasn't particularly happy about our trip, I assume none of his family was, but he came around once I told him I planned to test the change, and his trust being enough to satisfy the others, they agreed to let me leave. Not without him first fighting to come with me, of course, but this was something I needed to do myself.

Peering out the window, I speak low enough so the driver can't hear. "No, Adrian knows where we're going. He didn't believe my story for a second."

Elaine nods, wringing her hands between her knees nervously, glancing around at our surroundings every two minutes. She's been on edge ever since the night the hunters captured and almost killed me. "Do you ever think about Ambrose?"

Scoffing, I take a sip of the hot caramel latte I bought at the airport. I've never been a coffee drinker, but since my transition, I can't help but crave it when I get... hungry.

"Understatement of the century." I swallow, allowing the scorching liquid to burn my throat, though the sting doesn't last for long since my body fights constantly to heal and rejuvenate.

Elaine looks down at her lap, then up at me with eyes full of worry. "No, I meant about what he did to all of those people. Murdering them and then telling his family and the clans that he wanted to preserve humanity? It's repulsive."

"That's one word." Any time the topic of Ambrose is brought about in conversation, I become queasy. Talking about him allows thoughts of him into my head, subsequently letting him back into my mind, controlling my emotions and my thoughts. Fear and panic control me where he's concerned, and I refuse to give him that satisfaction from beyond the grave. Even dead, he has a power over me like no one else. "Saving humans was his sick way of justifying what he'd done. A life for a life. He craved ultimate control."

In a lot of ways, the clans inevitably protected the humans from him, not the other way around as he preached relentlessly up until the curse was placed on his family.

Elaine fumbles around in her purse, pulling out a stack of papers bursting from their small binding, not big enough to contain the stories printed within.

"Why do you carry that everywhere?" I ask, hating that she keeps such a thing with her at all times.

Now that I'm part of the Draven clan, I've come into a sort of wealth arrangement. The Twelve are almost like a government—they bring in money by doing business with the humans and then distribute it to the clan members. Being that Edgar Draven is one of the Twelve, he gets a fairly hefty paycheck that is divided between the members of his individual clan... which now includes me. I've used my share to remodel our house, subtly of course, so my parents wouldn't notice too many changes at once.

While redoing the hardwood upstairs, I came across the journal Ambrose must have kept while he was locked away in there two hundred years ago. I refuse to read it. I refuse to allow his story to go on after he spent most of my life controlling the emotions and actions of those around me. Elaine, on the other hand, was more than happy to get her hands on such an artifact.

She clears her throat, dragging her finger along the worn page as she reads a passage from the mind of a psychopath. "In his speech to the Twelve, he spoke, 'We were all human once, so we should respect their ways and their life force, protecting them so they can keep what we lost. Fore it should never be taken from them.'" It's her turn to scoff as she closes the journal, undoubtedly wondering why she bothered to open it. "What a load of crap."

"Do you think he ever believed that?"

"Maybe once." She shrugs limply, turning her attention to the small town coming into view. Home. "I've set up cameras around town. If any new faces pop up, I'll see them."

"Thanks, Elaine. For everything." We come to a stop, and she gets out of the cab.

"It's nothing." She smiles deviously, popping her head above the door before leaning back in. "Your knight awaits, madam."

"Bye, Elaine." I roll my eyes, turning as my door opens for me. Rising from the vehicle, I pay the driver and she pulls away, leaving my luggage—two small carry-ons and a ratty purse— lying in the middle of the street.

Miles pulls me into his arms, holding me by my slender waist.

"Welcome back," he breathes, placing his lips on my forehead. I wrap my arms around his shoulders and inhale deeply as I bury my face in his neck.

He releases me and lifts my bags from the pavement, slinging them over his shoulders. I smirk. "And they say chivalry is dead."

"I missed you, too." He bites his lip, looking off into the distance like he often does when he's thinking. I wait, knowing prodding him won't make his revelation come any faster. After a few moments, he finally says, "What if we just go?"

"Go?" I repeat, trying to read his expression. It's becoming easier the more I'm around him, but even still, I find it hard to believe I'll ever truly know what he's thinking. I'm undeniably certain Miles Draven will always be something of a mystery to me.

We walk slowly up the gravel pathway, stopping just beyond his home where his family and my brother sit outside, cooking something that smells marvelous on the grill. Dallas looks slightly out of place, but nonetheless more at ease with the Draven family. I'm just glad they agreed to watch out for him while I was gone.

Miles watches his siblings disconnectedly, turning his eyes back to me. "Not forever. Just… for a little while."

"And leave this all behind? Your family? Mine? Our responsibilities..."

"We'll compel your parents to think you're on a trip with some new friends, and as for your brother..." Miles glances at Dallas where he sits in an old woven lawn chair, frustrated with Vanesa because she can't accurately paint within the lines of the canvas he's drawn up for her. "Somehow I think he'll be just fine."

Miles holds out his arm and I latch on to it, wrapping my own around his and lacing our fingers together. My head fits perfectly against his shoulder and I suddenly find the idea of a vacation much more alluring. "As long as I'm back before school starts."

"You have forever in front of you and you want to waste it on a college education?" He shakes his head in bafflement of my logic.

"It keeps me grounded." That's not a complete lie. Doing human things helps keep me tethered to my humanity, which I don't want to lose. Where Ambrose failed in protecting the human race, I want to succeed. I believe wholeheartedly in his cause, a quality he clearly lacked, which means, if I decide to help the Dravens build an army—which I haven't—then I'll have the perfect opportunity to persuade others to see things my way.

"You've never had your feet on the ground, beautiful." Miles scoops me into his arms, luggage be damned, hugging me close.

None of us know what's coming next or if we'll be strong enough when it gets here. We'll be ready, though.

For most of my life, I was unprepared. Days and nights were spent wishing on stars and dreaming up fantasies because I wanted more than what life handed me. There were times I thought I'd spend my entire life looking for what I'd never find. I wanted so many things for myself that I feared I'd spend forever wishing I had, and then suddenly, I woke up one day and the life I'd stumbled upon was enough to satisfy my endeavoring desires. I found myself, and what's more, I discovered my purpose. And I'm not talking about Miles. I may have found love along the way, but what matters most is because of his life crashing into mine, I gained so much more than an ordinary love and a wasteful purpose, not stuck yet never quite going anywhere. That's how I felt for most of my short and unimpressionable existence. Useless. Until now.

Because no matter what happens from here, at least I'm alive.

And living is exponentially better than dying.

WANT MORE OF THE DRAVEN FAMILY?

Keep reading for a sneak peek of book two in the Nightfall
series, **In the Moonlight.**

IN THE MOONLIGHT

CHAPTER ONE

Water drips down my arms as I stand beneath the rain-soaked tree, the branches creaking softly against the chilly air. There's no movement in sight except for a small group of kids creeping steadily up the hill, as far as they dare wander for fear of being seen. The girl leans in close to one of the boys, softly whispering in his ear. He snickers giddily, nodding in approval. The girl then turns to the other, looking ahead.

"You should touch it," the girl says, cupping a hand over her mouth in a silent giggle. They can't be more than twelve—maybe thirteen.

The second boy turns, glancing between his friends hesitantly and then shakes his head. "You mean the gate?"

A sly grin stretches across the girl's face as her gaze travels up the iron posts glimmering in the moonlight. "Better yet... ring the doorbell."

"Maria..." he drags out her name, fumbling with the hem of his t-shirt and glancing over his shoulder at the tall mansion ahead. The three of them are hidden in the night's cover for now, but a few more feet and the spotlights shining on the length of the Manor will bathe them in light. "You can't be serious."

She rests an elbow on the shoulder of the boy next to her. "I mean, if you're too scared…"

"I'm not," he says immediately, clearing his throat.

"Then do it," she coaxes, and the first boy lets out a strangled noise.

"I'm not sure that's such a good idea. The gate is one thing… but what if they're awake?"

"Then we'd better run like hell," Maria responds, egging him on. "I dare you."

The second boy looks behind him once again, assessing the height he must climb in order to fulfill his dare. "I'll need a leg up."

The three stumble to the gate, crouching down to avoid being seen. Just as they begin to hoist him up, a fourth shadow appears behind them, towering over their thin bodies.

The kids turn slowly, eyes wide and fearful. The girl shoves the two boys in front of her, then dashes back down the hill faster than her feet can carry her. She trips, stumbling and rolling the rest of the way. The boys stand, shaking in fear as the figure closes in on them. Cracking his neck, the figure moves closer and his deep voice cuts through the silence like a knife.

"Leave."

"Y-yes, sir," one of the boys stutters, latching on to the arm of the other, pulling him in the same direction as Maria.

My eyes slice through the dark, taking in the figure as he smirks darkly, watching them retreat, tripping and shoving, stumbling over each other and their own limbs. Then he turns, and in an instant, he's in front of me. His sinister smile stays cemented in place until his eyes travel to my bare toes, submerged in a shallow pool of muddy leaves and rainwater.

"What are you doing out here?" Miles asks finally. Leaning against the tree, he crosses his arms, eyes roaming over me.

"Watching," I say simply, looking back to the path the kids used to run away. Now they have their own stories to tell. Their own contribution to the town's plethora of tall tales about the Draven family and the horrors that lie beyond the safety of town. I scoff at that thought. *Safety.* Whoever believes such a lie must know better than to go into town after dark, because I know firsthand the true horrors that lurk in the shadows of this damning place.

Miles breathes in, tracing a warm finger down my cheek and across my jawline where he pauses on my bottom lip, triggering a wave of goose bumps that travel across my damp skin.

"You'll get pneumonia," he whispers, entranced by something about me that I can't see.

I roll my eyes, even as I rub my hands over my arms. "No, I won't."

I thought becoming a vampire would make me numb, cold, heartless, and immune to all of the weaknesses humans are programmed with. But I can still feel the cold, and the warmth of another's skin. I can feel pain, although it dissipates rather quickly. And I feel hunger so intense it burns in my gut and claws at me from the inside out until I satisfy it with the blood it craves. Most people are ruled by love, envy, or hate. The lucky few have minds so strong they can keep themselves from becoming overwhelmed by all of those emotions—they can compartmentalize and decipher them rationally, logically. But me? I'm ruled by the utmost desire to devour anything that stands between me and my next meal.

I don't get sick, though. I'll never age, nor will I ever die so long as my life isn't stolen from me first. Eternity sits before me on a pedestal, and I don't have the first clue of what to do with it.

"I'll never have kids," I say abruptly. "I mean, I never knew if I wanted them—I'd never really given it much thought to be honest—but now I know I'll never have kids."

The choice was made for me, like so many others.

I meet his eyes then, bright as the stars above us, their color resembling that of the moon's. Yet, there's an abyss of darkness there as well, an inhuman part that stays hidden behind the light. He closes them, momentarily snuffing out their glow. "I never wanted this for you."

"I'll never make new friends, either," I continue absentmindedly, turning into the breeze to remove the hair from my face. "I can't. After so long, they'll realize I'm not aging. And the friends I have now, and my family—I'll be forced to watch them grow old and die. Leaving me here. Alone. I potentially have more life ahead of me than every human in this world combined, and I feel like it's already over."

Well, either that, or I'll die before my life has even begun. Because in this twisted world, there are no assurances.

Miles dips his chin, lowering his gaze to find mine in the dark, and takes my face gently in his warm hands. "So long as I'm alive, you will never be alone, beautiful."

"You don't know that," I whisper, feeling a burn in my nose.

Before I turned, one of my biggest fears was losing myself to the monster within. But now I am the monster.

"I do." He presses a kiss to my temple, pulling me in until I'm wrapped in his arms and my entire body is pressed so tight to him that it suppresses my trembling. All of my apprehensions melt away in his embrace as I focus on the sound of our hearts beating as one. "I promise you, Aspen Troy, no matter what happens in this lifetime, or the next, loneliness will never find you."

"Unless Vanesa locks me in a cage and siphons venom from my veins," I say without humor.

Vanesa is still angry with me for refusing to build her family an army to fight the other clans, and once the Twelve discover I've broken the curse that was placed on the Dravens, they'll attack with the sole purpose of wiping us out.

Miles' shoulders shake with laughter, and he pulls back to look at my face, placing a kiss on the bridge of my nose, then each cheek and my chin, before his cold lips find mine. He brushes them temptingly, allowing his bottom lip to scrape across mine before molding them together and sliding his hands down my stomach and around my back, pressing me into him.

He breaks away, sucking in a sharp breath, and lifts me onto a low-hanging tree branch so I'm slightly above him in height. His fingers play with the holes in my jeans, worn from long and tiring days and nights of fighting, training, pushing myself to the brink of death, sleeping, then starting all over again. I'm luckier than most newborns since I had a little bit of self-defense training before I turned. If only it had been enough to keep me alive.

Miles slips his hand beneath the ripped fabric on my knee,

tracing around the hole with his thumb. "You know, just because you can't have kids doesn't mean we can't help young vampires find their way."

I nod solemnly, unable to let go of all the things this life was supposed to bring me before death. Instead, it brought me death before I'd hardly lived.

IN THE MOONLIGHT

CHAPTER TWO

The floor creaks beneath my feet as I tiptoe across the living room, reaching carefully over my father's snoring figure for the remote to turn down the TV. A quick chill races through the room and I tremble, looking for the source. This time, unlike most of the others, there is a reasonable explanation for the draft, and it's the open window over the kitchen sink. Since I killed Ambrose Draven, the paranormal activity in my house has stopped, but no matter how many times I scrub the floors, he's still here, still watching me, still waiting for the perfect moment to strike. I don't think I'll live a day of my life without remembering the feel of his fingers on my skin, his tongue tracing the line of my veins.

My stomach churns at the memories, and I reach for the window, preparing to close it when it slams shut on its own. I jump back, spinning around and checking every dark corner for glowing eyes. I wait for the feeling of his breath on my neck, or his voice to whisper my name, but it never comes. The only thing I hear is my father groaning as he sits up, rubbing his eyes.

"Aspen?" He peers at me through the dark. It's almost impossible for him to see me in this light, but I can see him. He twists around, looking for the flashlight that never leaves his side, almost as if he's afraid of the dark.

Elliot made sure my parents wouldn't remember a thing about what happened the night Ambrose attacked, and they don't. But they must know something bad happened, something worse than what we told them so they'd be able to sleep at night and allow us to leave the house without worrying. Because now they're always paranoid. Almost like they can't see what it is they're supposed to be afraid of, but they know it's there, watching, waiting.

"I'm over here." I give in before he turns on his flashlight and blows my cover. Our power went out last night, and even Ted, the town handyman, can't seem to figure out why. Now only the TV and kitchen appliances are connected to a small generator out back.

Father's head swivels in my direction, and he flinches, clicking on the flashlight anyway.

"Sorry, did I wake you?"

He shakes his head, looking at me strangely. "No, I don't think so." He purses his lips, shining the light on my face before shaking his head again, running a hand over his face. "That was weird. For a minute, it looked like your eyes were glowing."

"Probably a trick of the light." I gesture toward the TV, shifting so my dirty feet are hidden from view. I rummage through the pantry in search of something sugary to curb my cravings. The only reason I left my house tonight was to get something to eat, but I was distracted by the kids sneaking up to Draven Manor, and then by Miles, and I didn't realize until I walked through the door that I'm still absolutely famished.

"Shouldn't we at least talk about what happened?" he asks, taking a few swigs of water from the glass sitting beside him. Apparently, it was Ambrose's influence that drove my father to drink and made my mom retreat into herself. When we took away their memories of him, it also took away their memories of who they became during that time. Ambrose told me once that he couldn't make a monster out of a good man... does that mean the people my parents became is something they're truly capable of? Is it possible for my father to really be *that* mean all the time?

"What's to talk about?" I shrug him off, grabbing a box of something that looks like a chocolate dessert—cupcakes maybe? He won't let it go. Almost every time he sees me, he brings it up. "A man broke into our house. Tried to kill me. You and Mom ran. Dallas and I scared him away. There's nothing left to say."

I walk quickly to my bedroom, slamming the door before he has the chance to say anything else. It's hard enough having to lie, having to downplay everything bad that's happened to me over the past few months, but what's worse is constantly worrying about slipping up and revealing a new piece of information that we haven't programmed them to know. In order to make them forget Ambrose, Elliot had to *make* them remember something else. He couldn't just erase such a traumatic experience and convince them they were sleeping the whole time—which I would have preferred. He had to implement parts of the truth. Personally, I wish we could ship them back to Colorado like this never happened. But nothing is ever that simple.

"You're awake?" I mumble, noticing my brother sitting up in bed, sketchpad in hand, flashlight in his lap. I move away from the empty doorframe between our rooms, and strip out of my wet clothes, throwing on an old nightgown and slipping under my covers. I then unwrap a mini cupcake and plop it in my mouth, savoring the sweet chocolate.

Dallas doesn't flinch, hardly acknowledging my presence. "I don't sleep anymore."

Guilt pricks in my heart, expanding in my chest. Dallas used to have horrible dreams, so bad that I'd have to stay up the entire night just to make sure his screams didn't wake up our parents. But now... now that my brother has had a glimpse behind the curtain, a peek into the world of blood and horror, he can't sleep at all. Ambrose invading his dreams didn't do him any favors, but I can't help but feel like everything that's happened is somehow my fault. The only reason I don't resent Miles for finding me, saving me, turning me into what I am, is because if it weren't for him, I'd be dead. Dallas likes to pretend he's angry, that he's terrified that his life has forever changed. But if he had lost me, too, after our own brother tried to kill us because drugs were more important to him, it would have quite literally ruined him.

"I think Father is starting to remember." I sigh, pressing my face into a pillow. "Or he just knows something feels wrong."

Elliot originally used a temporary memory potion to make them forget what happened with Ambrose, and then eventually used his compulsion, which doesn't seem to be up to par.

Dallas grunts, and I hear his pencil drop to his sketchpad. He's quiet for a long while until he finally speaks. "Everything is wrong."

"Dallas—"

"Why couldn't you make me forget, too?"

I clear my throat, staring up at the ceiling as his words

strike me. I let them seep into my skin, wrap around my bones, and suffocate my heart. "I didn't know you wanted that."

"I don't, I guess. I'd just much rather go back to being afraid of the dark—*only* the dark."

"Not what lies beyond it," I whisper. "I'm sorry. All I ever wanted was to protect you."

"Maybe that's the problem," he says without a trace of emotion in his tone as he shifts on his old mattress. We decided to keep the crappy ones for the time being, at least until the more pressing issues with the house are tended to. Although, no amount of fixing is going to make this place livable again. We'd probably be better off tearing it down and building a new house from the bottom up.

I don't respond to his offhand comment. With Derek unhinged and on the other side of the world, and our parents basically incapacitated, the two of us only have each other. But lately, I feel even our relationship is dwindling. How long do I have until my own flesh and blood becomes a stranger I faintly recognize?

An odd smell drags me from sleep. I scrunch my nose and attempt to roll on my side to see if I left the window open, but when I try to move, I notice a heavy weight pressing down on me. I shift, left then right, but I'm pinned in place by what feels like a body pushing down on me.

The smell grows stronger, burning my nose and souring my stomach so much so that I feel as if I might puke. And then the tapping starts. I can't see where it's coming from, but it's consistent and grows louder each time I struggle to sit up.

I cry out, the air in my lungs growing thinner and thinner as the heaviness increases. The pressure builds until I'm wheezing.

"You can't escape," a voice growls. A finger drags across my collarbone to the collar of my shirt, then up my neck to the permanent mark reminding me of the day my life forever changed. I can't see him, but I can feel him—and not just physically. He's in every fabric of my being, in my pores and in my veins like a drug. I feel his hot breath and then the touch of a cold tongue across my ear. "You will never escape me."

ALSO BY LEXI J. KINGSTON

Nightfall Series

Come Nightfall

In the Moonlight

Until Daybreak

After Sunrise

If you're interested in romantic comedy/sweet romance, check out my other titles under Lexi Kingston:

13 Days of December series

Remember December

Endure May

Trusting November

Forever June

ABOUT THE AUTHOR

Lexi (J.) Kingston started writing when she was fifteen years old solely because she was obsessed with the idea of creating fictional worlds like the ones she lived through growing up. There was this thrilling allure to writing characters that you can relate to and find pieces of yourself within that she couldn't shake, and this eventually drew her to fiction writing. She wanted to create a world people could get lost in—a fictional safe haven, if you will. A place filled with endless possibilities, where you can lose yourself, yet find yourself within the pages.

You can find Lexi's contemporary romance titles under "Lexi Kingston."

LEXI KINGSTON ONLINE:
INSTAGRAM: instagram.com/l.kingston.books
FACEBOOK: fb.me/l.kingston.books
TWITTER: twitter.com/Lkingston_books
BOOKBUB: bookbub.com/profile/lexi-kingston
WEBSITE: https://lkingstonbooks.com